BY MICHAEL HARDCASTLE

ILLUSTRATED BY MICHAEL REID
COLORS BY JESSICA FUCHS

W9-CFJ-351

Librarian Reviewer
Laurie K. Holland
Media Specialist (National Board Certified), Edina, MN
MA in Elementary Education, Minnesota State University, Mankato, MN

Reading Consultant
Sherry Klehr
Elementary/Middle School Educator, Edina Public Schools, MN
MA in Education, University of Minnesota, MN

STONE ARCH BOOKS
Minneapolis   San Diego

First published in the United States in 2006
by Stone Arch Books,
A Capstone Imprint
151 Good Counsel Drive, P.O. Box 669,
Mankato, Minnesota 56002.
www.capstonepub.com

Originally published in Great Britain in 2002
by A & C Black Publishers Ltd,
38 Soho Square, London, W1D 3HB.

Library of Congress Cataloging-in-Publication Data
Hardcastle, Michael.
    Archie's Amazing Game / by Michael Hardcastle; illustrated by Michael Reid.
    p. cm. — (Graphic Trax)
    ISBN-13: 978-1-59889-025-9 (library binding)
    ISBN-10: 1-59889-025-5 (library binding)
    ISBN-13: 978-1-59889-175-1 (paperback)
    ISBN-10: 1-59889-175-8 (paperback)
    1. Graphic novels. I. Reid, Michael, Illustrator II. Title. III. Series.
PN6727.H375A73 2006
741.5—dc22   2005026690

Summary: Archie loves playing soccer, but his mother has banned him from playing
during their vacation. He makes clever agreements with his brother and sister,
hoping he'll be able to play.

Printed in the United States of America in Stevens Point, Wisconsin.
122009
005645R

TABLE OF CONTENTS

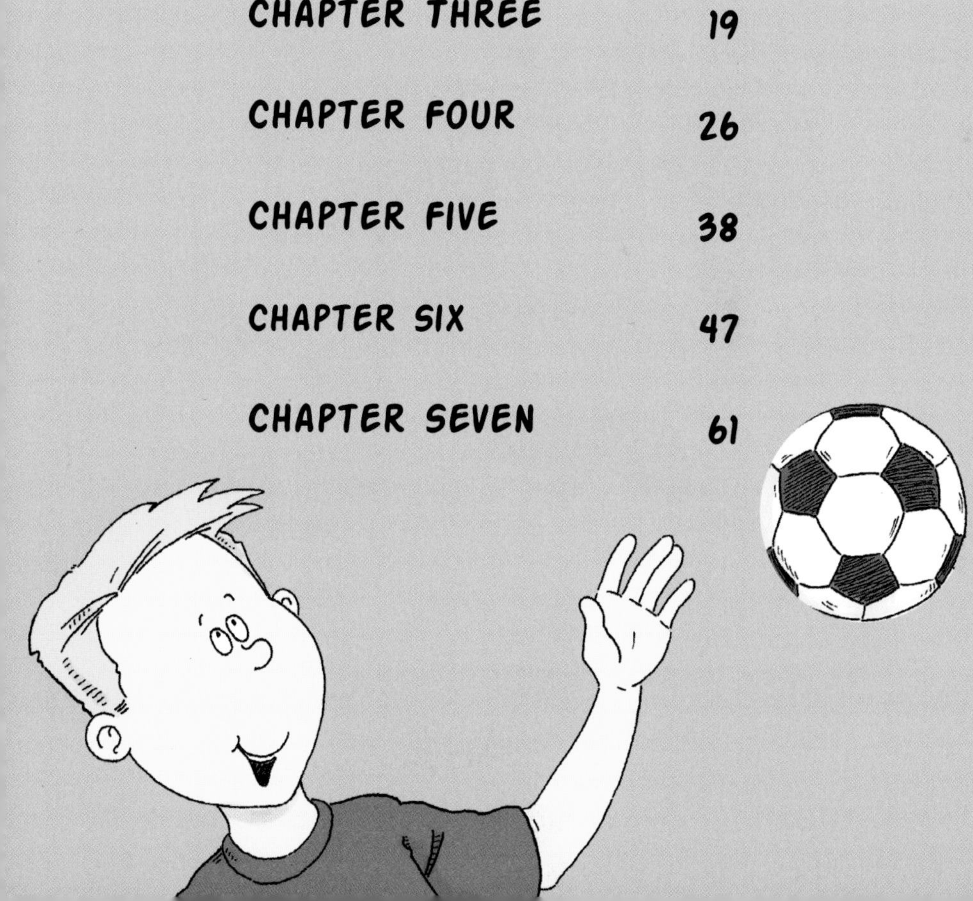

CAST OF CHARACTERS

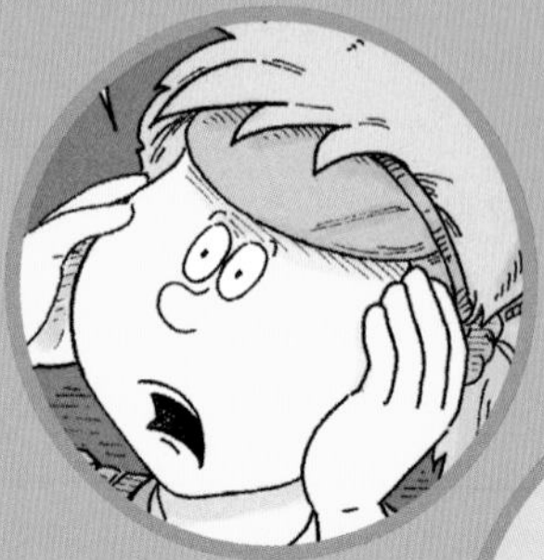

JENNY

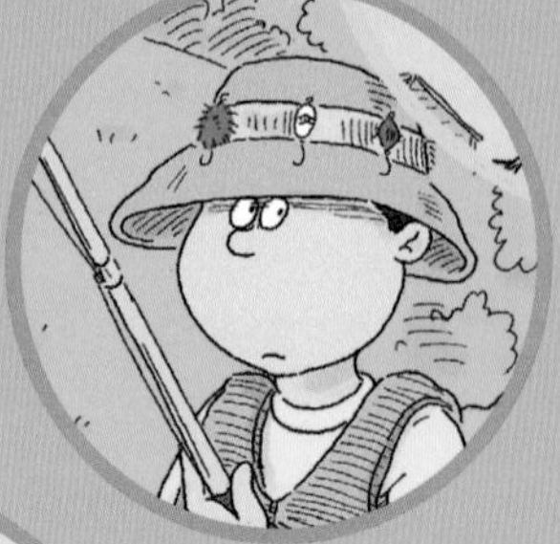

ROSS

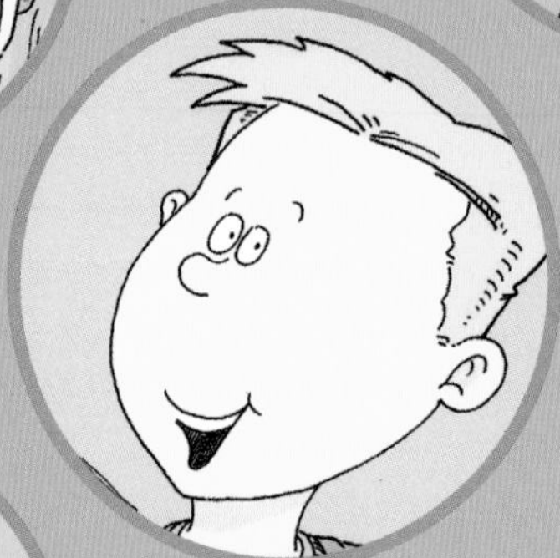

ARCHIE

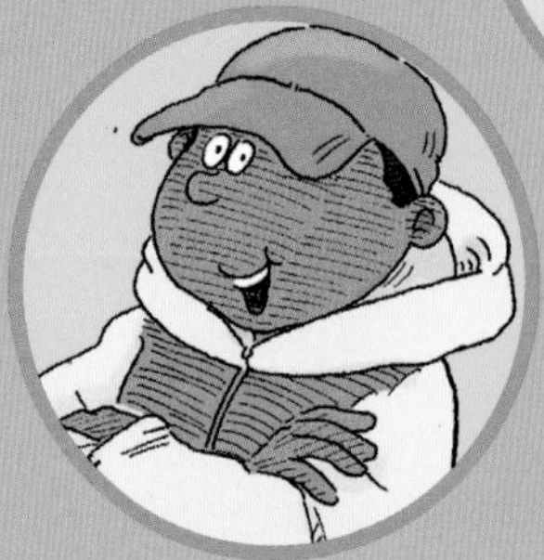

KYLE

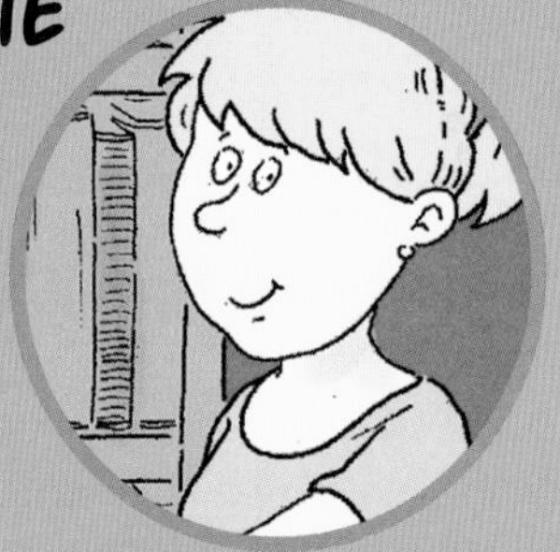

ARCHIE'S MOM

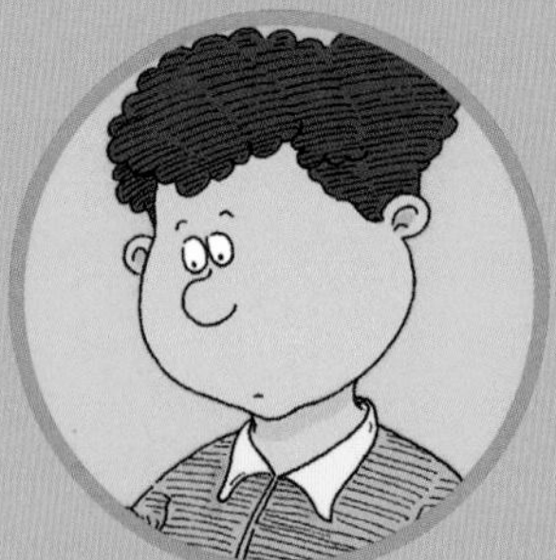

TOM

CHAPTER ONE

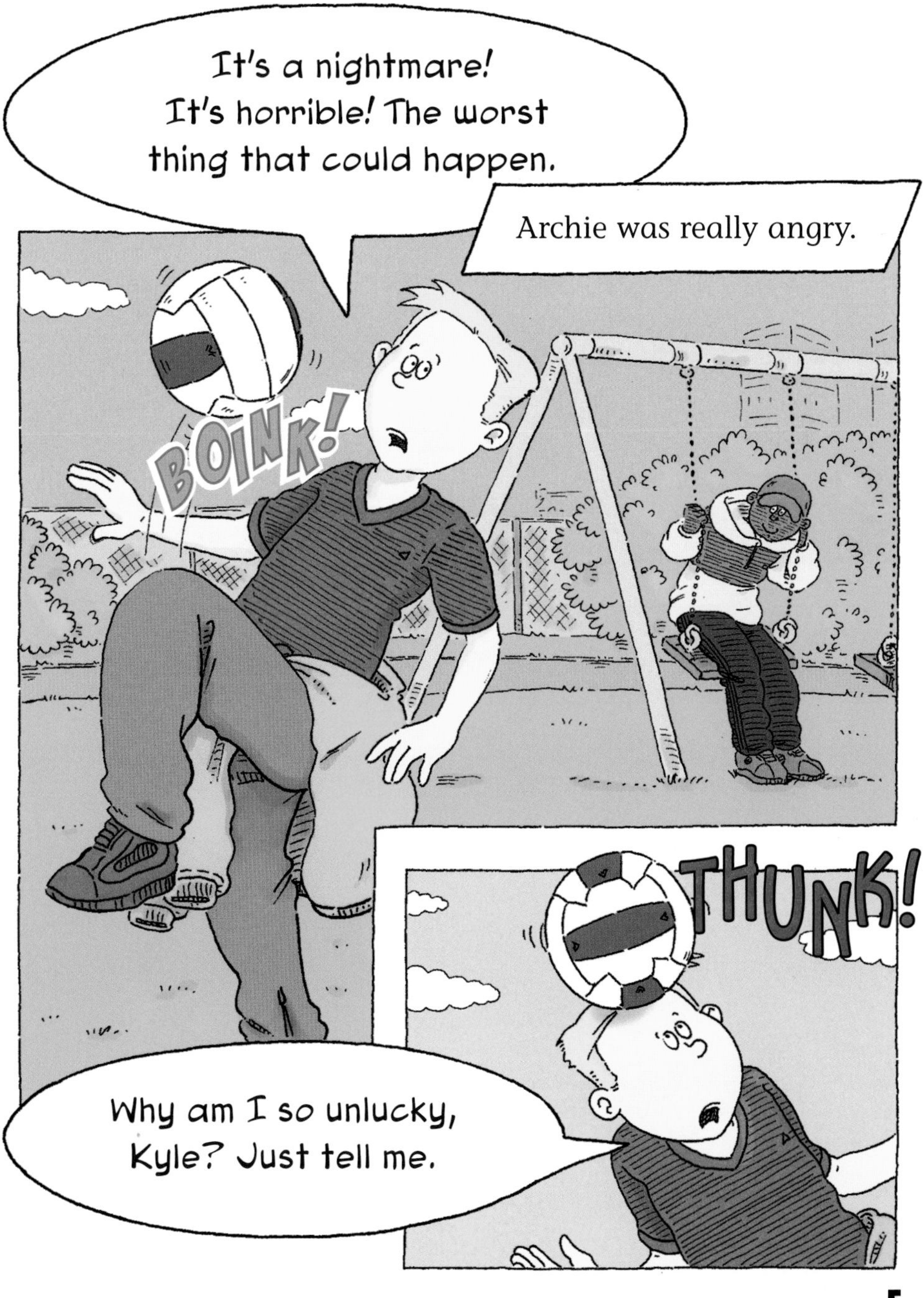
It's a nightmare! It's horrible! The worst thing that could happen.
Archie was really angry.
BOINK!
THUNK!
Why am I so unlucky, Kyle? Just tell me.

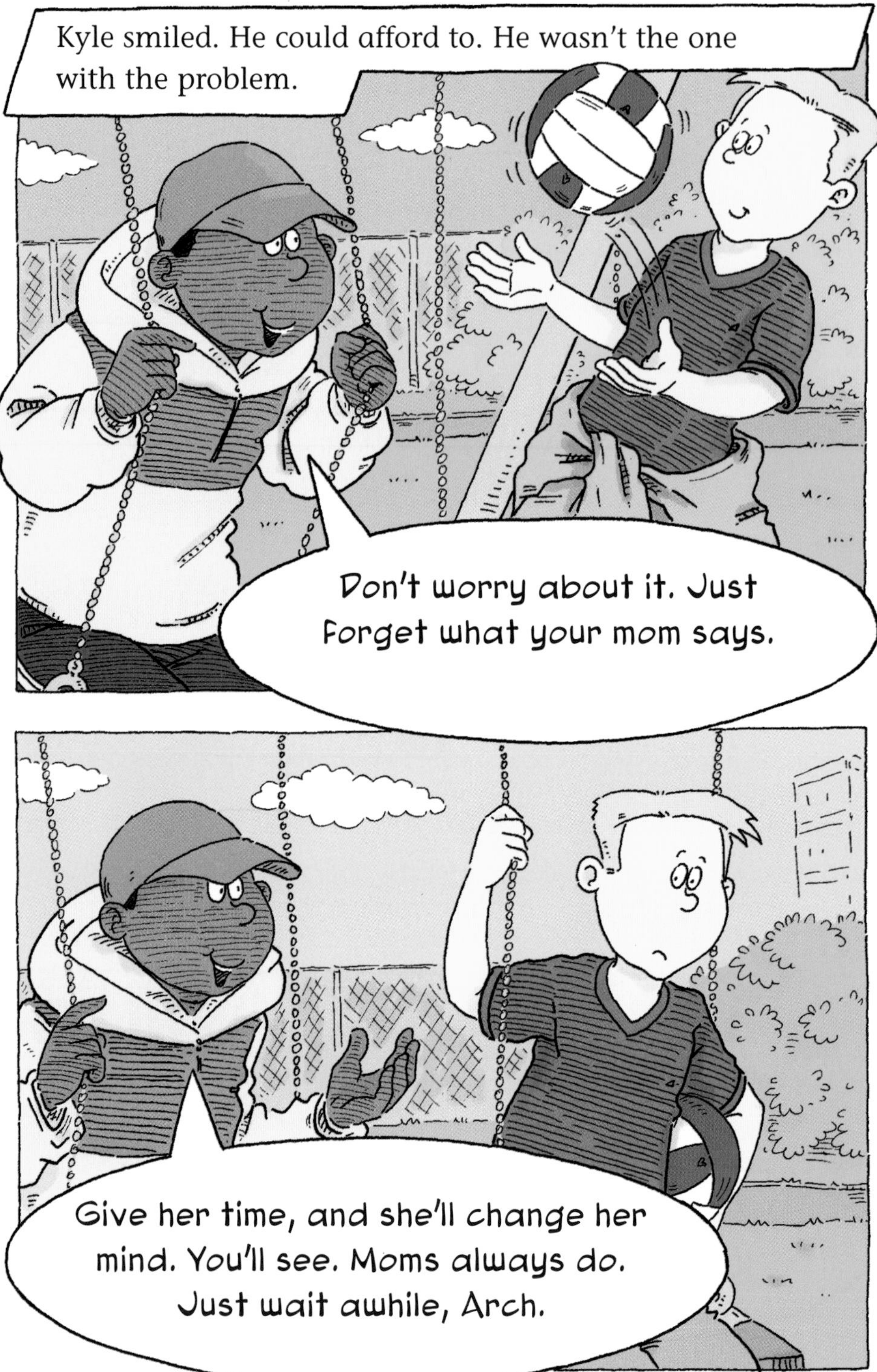
Kyle smiled. He could afford to. He wasn't the one with the problem.
Don't worry about it. Just forget what your mom says.
Give her time, and she'll change her mind. You'll see. Moms always do. Just wait awhile, Arch.

Archie expected Kyle to offer some useful advice instead of telling him to do nothing at all. Maybe Kyle didn't understand how big of a problem his mom's ban on soccer was.

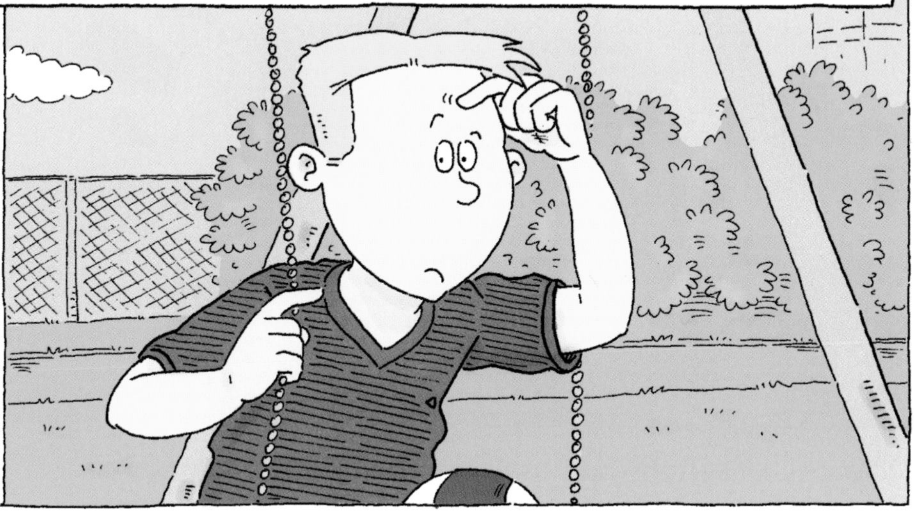

Kyle was sitting on the park swing, arms wrapped around the chains and looking as if he were in a dream.

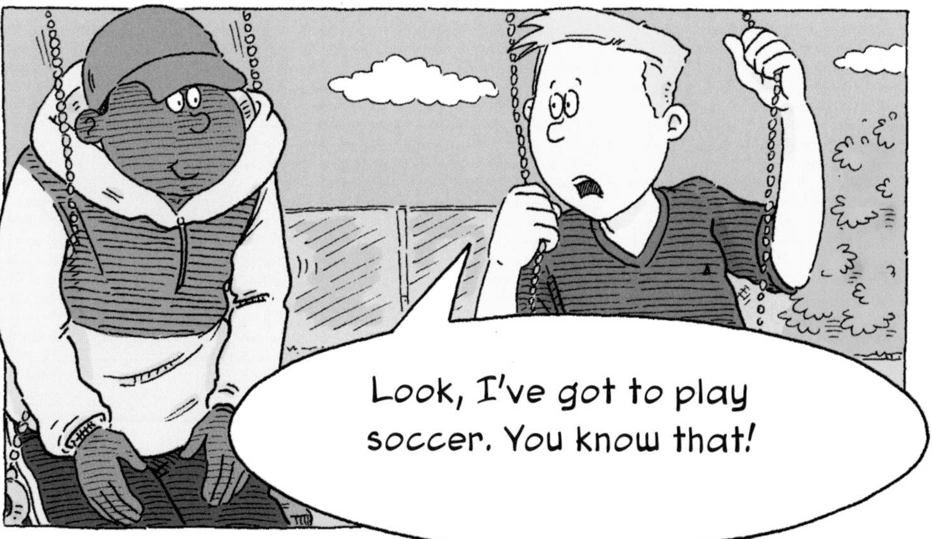
Look, I've got to play soccer. You know that!

As if to prove it, Archie began bouncing the ball on his left foot. He flipped it to his right foot.

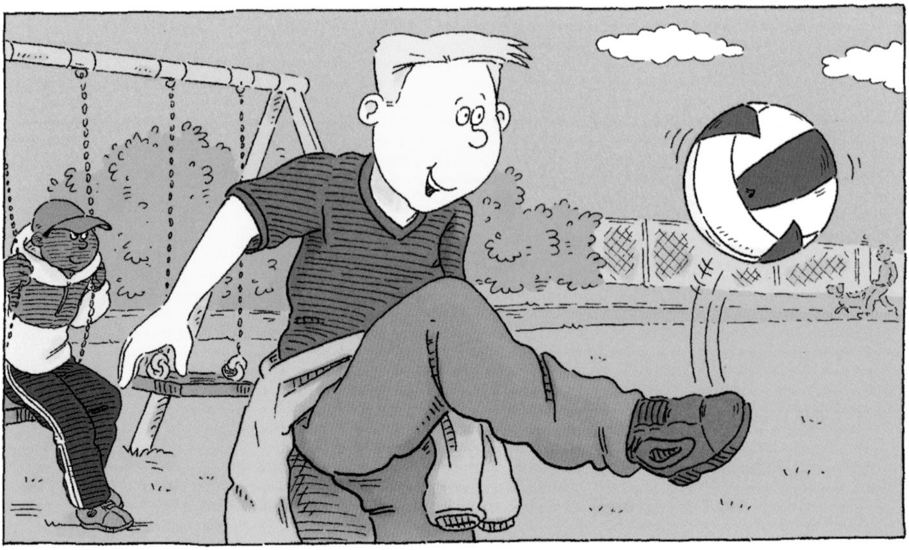

Then he kicked the ball high into the air. On its way down, he caught it on the back of his neck before letting it roll down his sloping back to the ground.

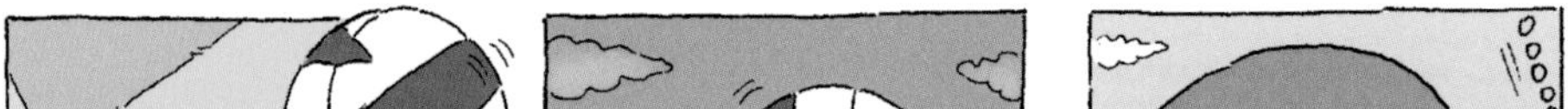
SMACK!

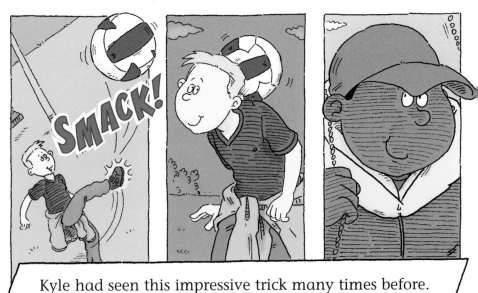

Kyle had seen this impressive trick many times before.

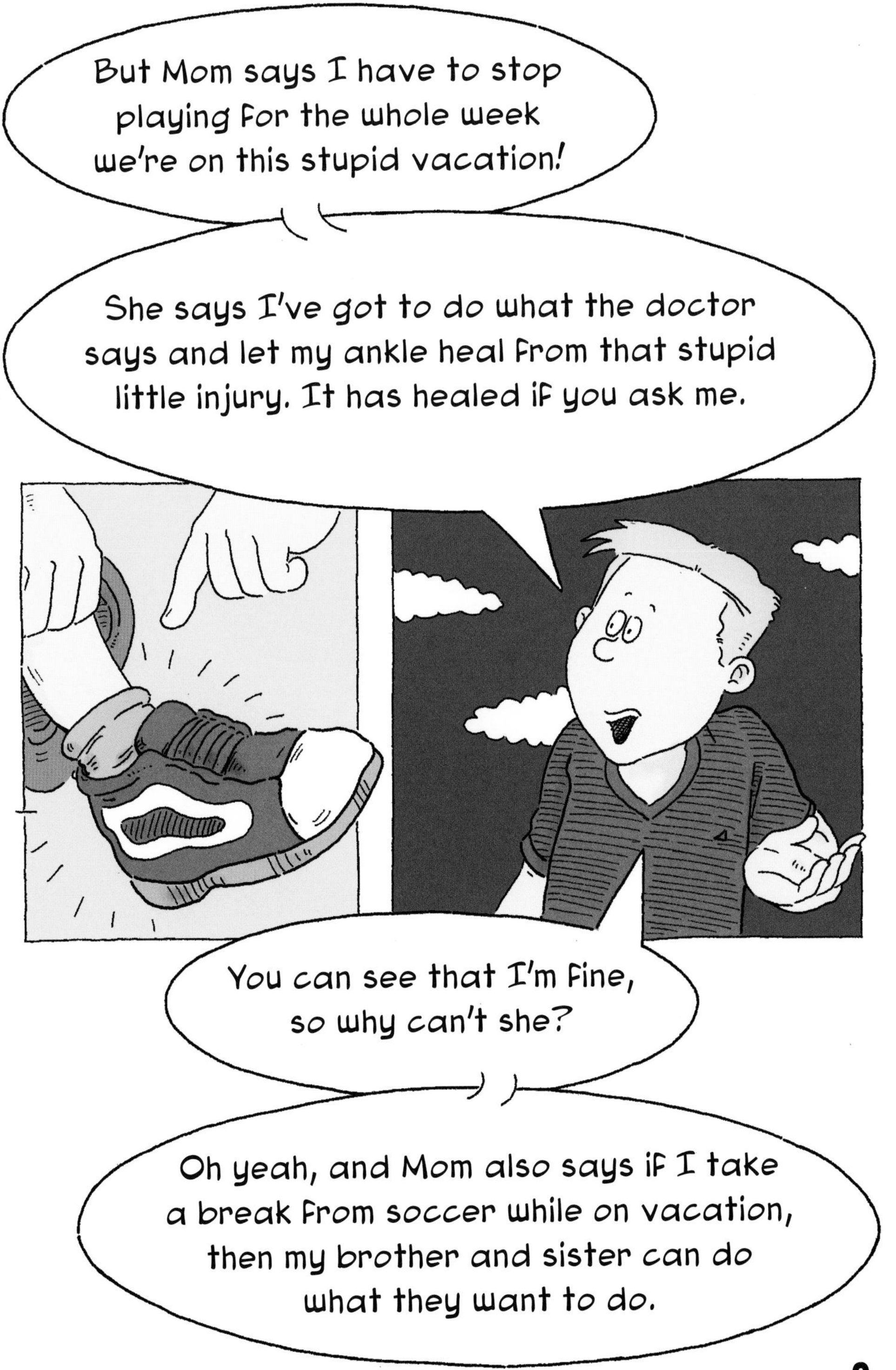
But Mom says I have to stop playing for the whole week we're on this stupid vacation!
She says I've got to do what the doctor says and let my ankle heal from that stupid little injury. It has healed if you ask me.
You can see that I'm fine, so why can't she?
Oh yeah, and Mom also says if I take a break from soccer while on vacation, then my brother and sister can do what they want to do.

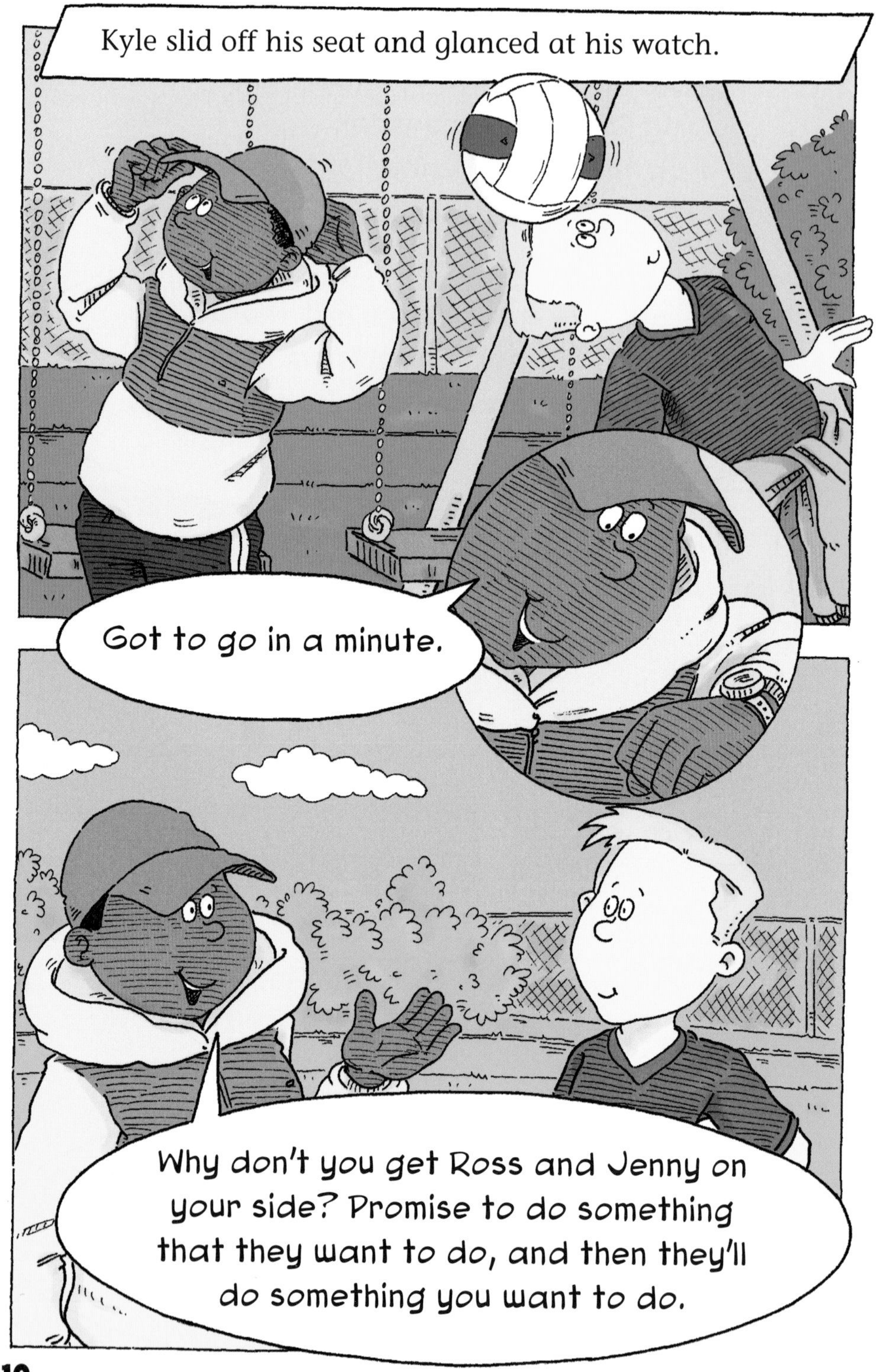
Kyle slid off his seat and glanced at his watch.
Got to go in a minute.
Why don't you get Ross and Jenny on your side? Promise to do something that they want to do, and then they'll do something you want to do.

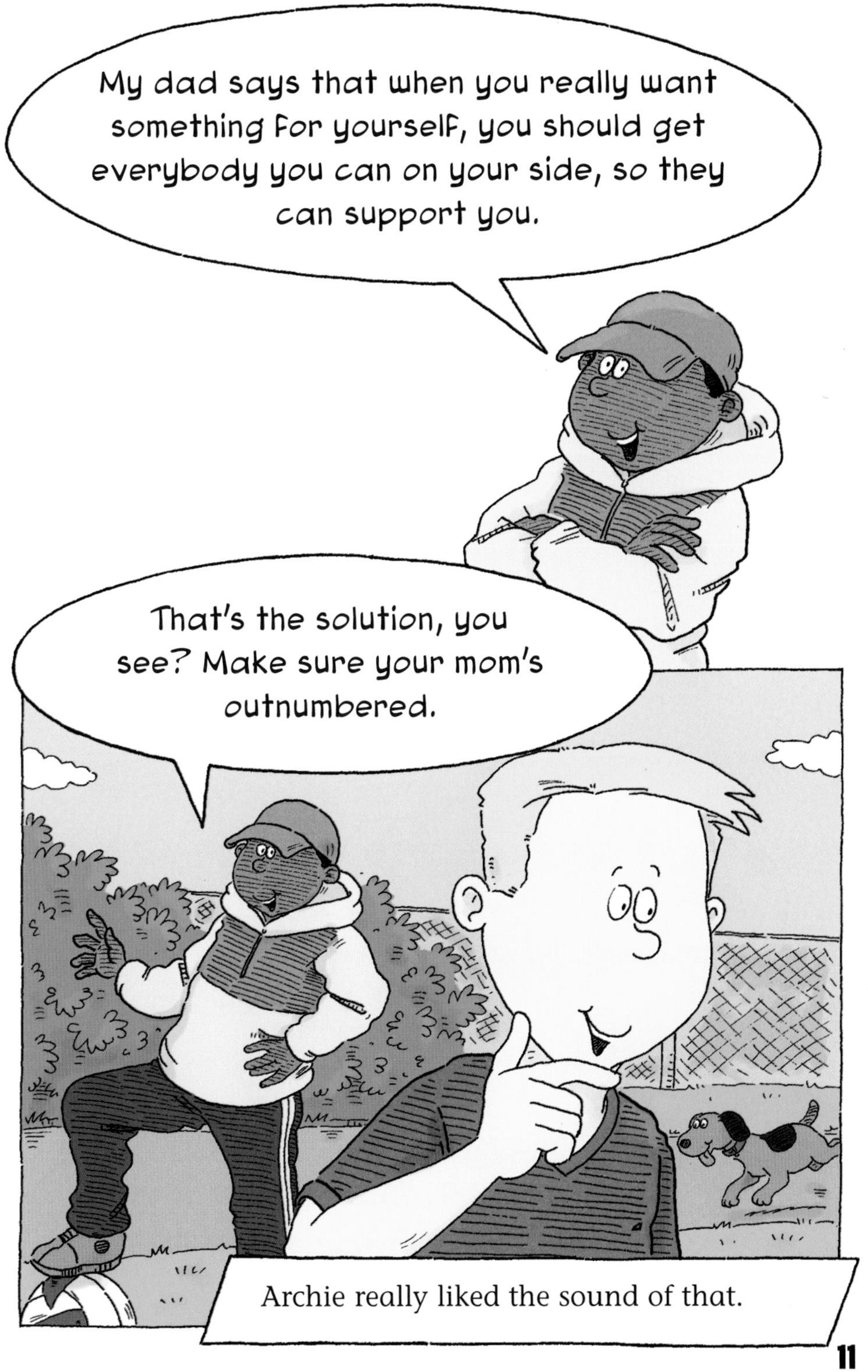
My dad says that when you really want something for yourself, you should get everybody you can on your side, so they can support you.
That's the solution, you see? Make sure your mom's outnumbered.
Archie really liked the sound of that.

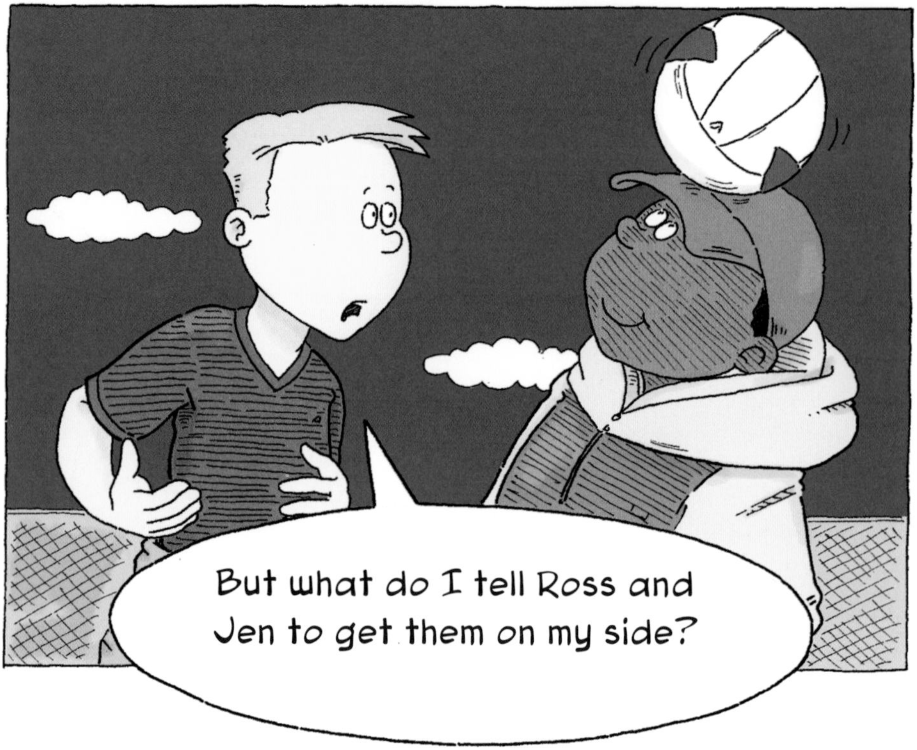
But what do I tell Ross and Jen to get them on my side?

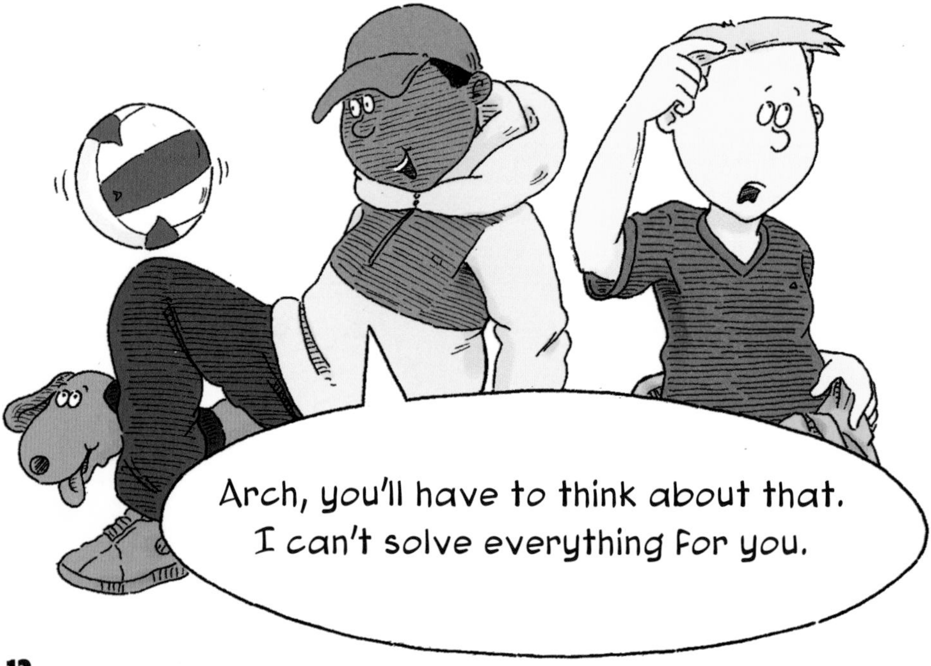
Arch, you'll have to think about that. I can't solve everything for you.

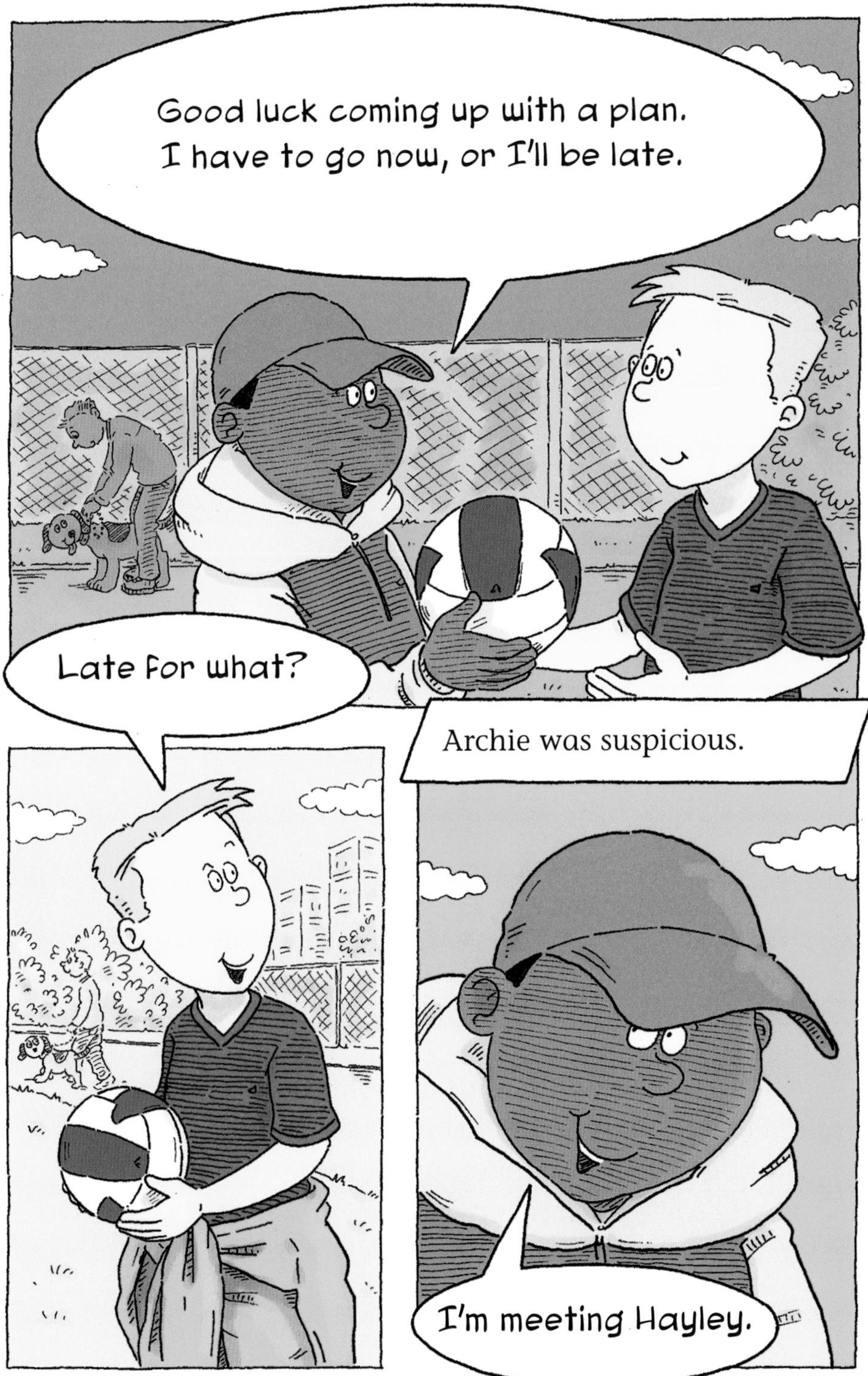
Good luck coming up with a plan.
I have to go now, or I'll be late.
Late for what?
Archie was suspicious.
I'm meeting Hayley.

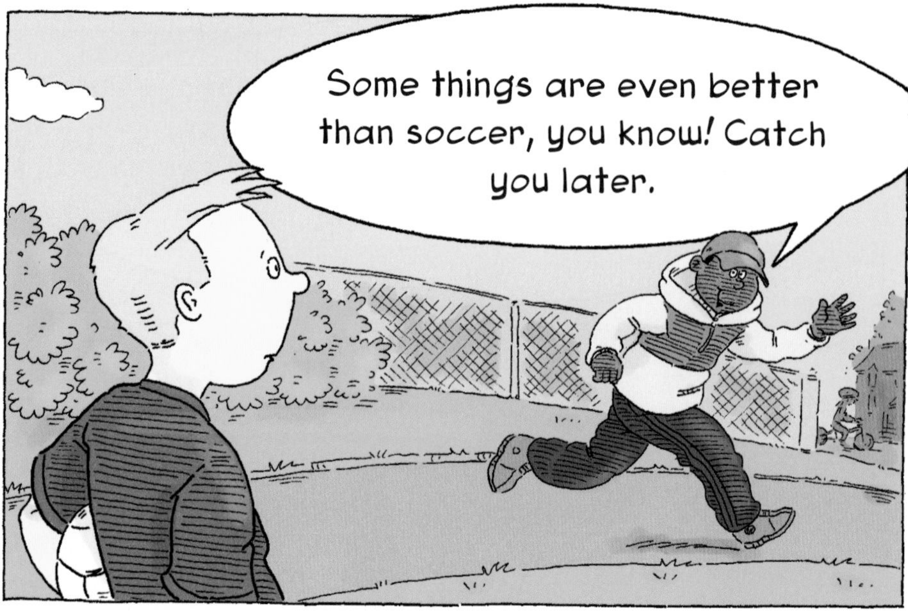
Some things are even better than soccer, you know! Catch you later.

"Oh, girls," muttered Archie as his best friend darted across the park.

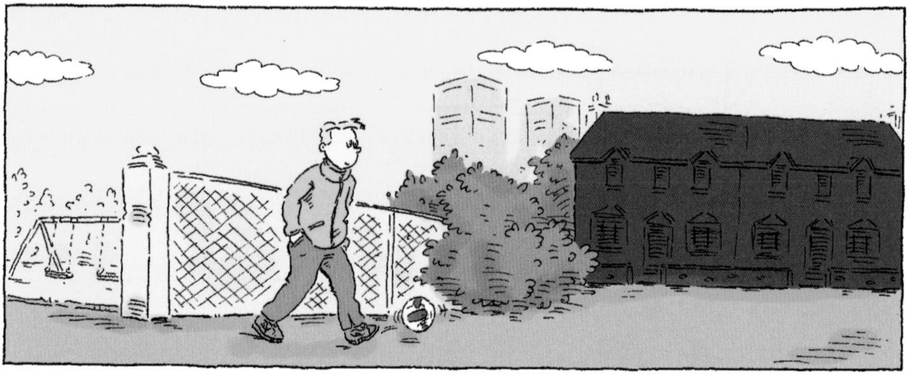

Archie's head was filled with thoughts of how he could get his brother and sister to help him when the family went on vacation to Carnegie Park next week. He couldn't come up with anything better than Kyle's suggestion.

CHAPTER TWO

Archie's mom was lying on the couch in the living room, reading a book. It was a familiar sight because she loved reading. She believed that just about everything in life could be learned from a book.

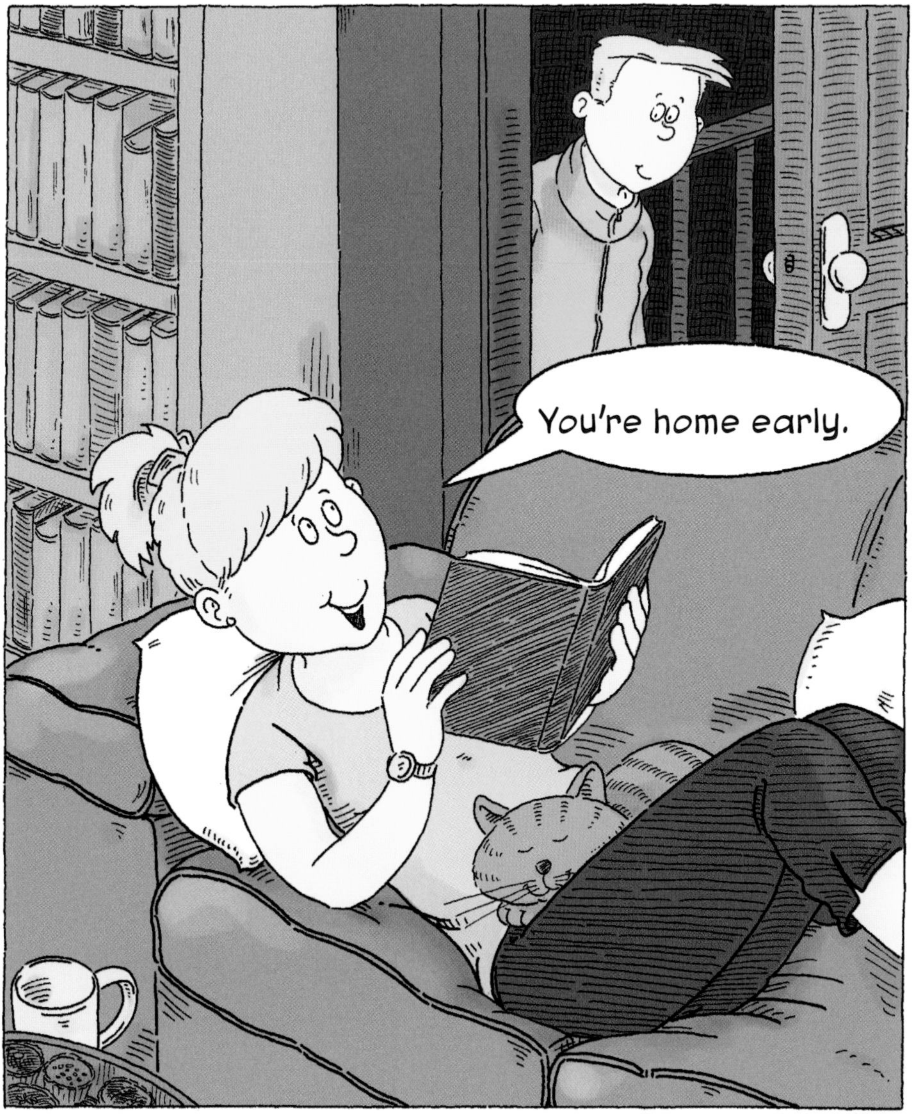
You're home early.

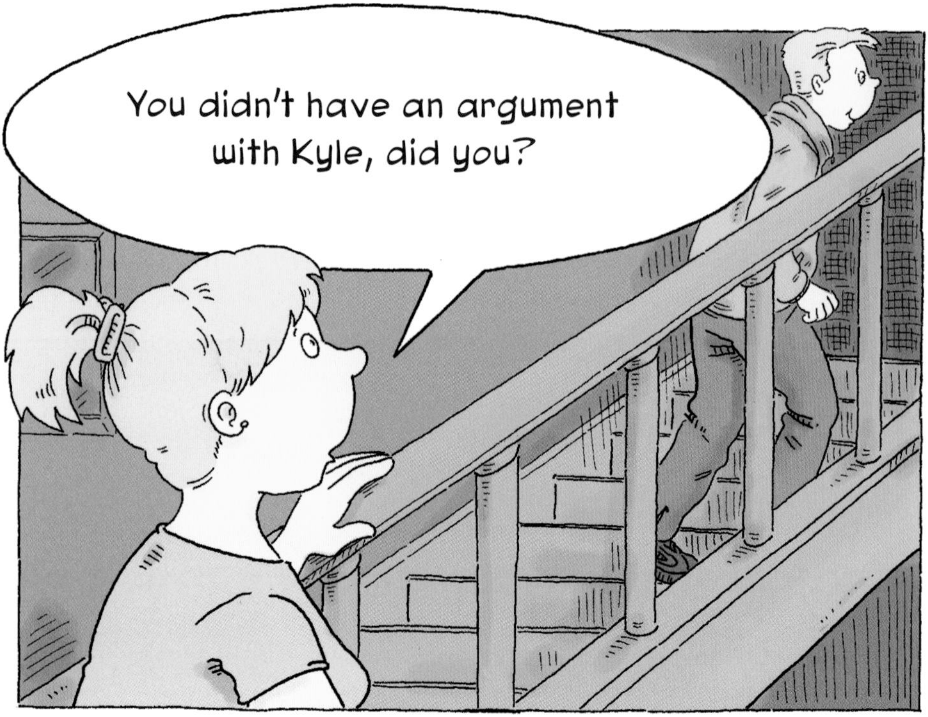
You didn't have an argument with Kyle, did you?

She knew her oldest son had a quick temper at times.

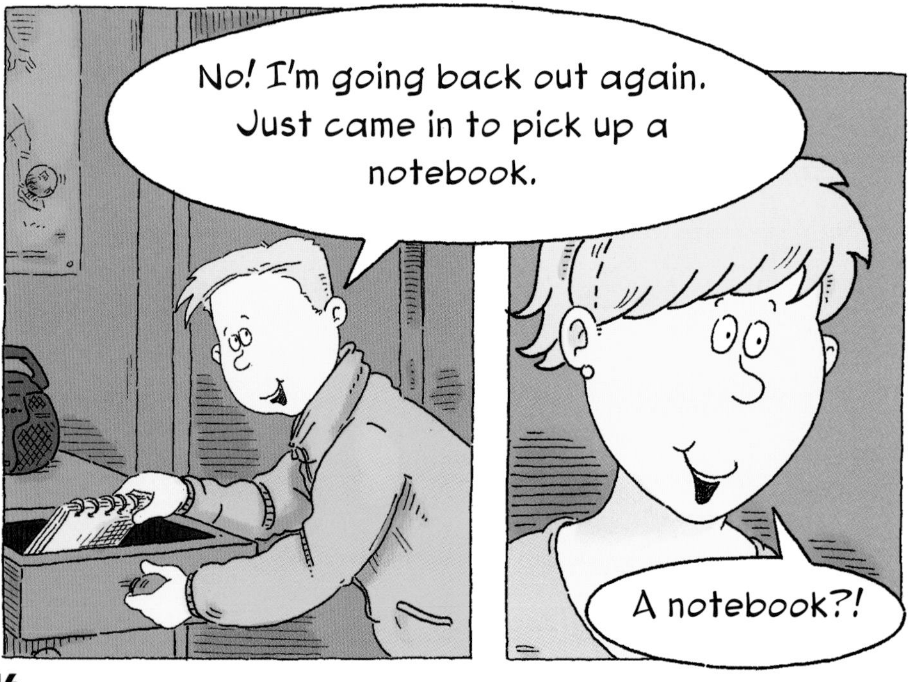
No! I'm going back out again. Just came in to pick up a notebook.
A notebook?!

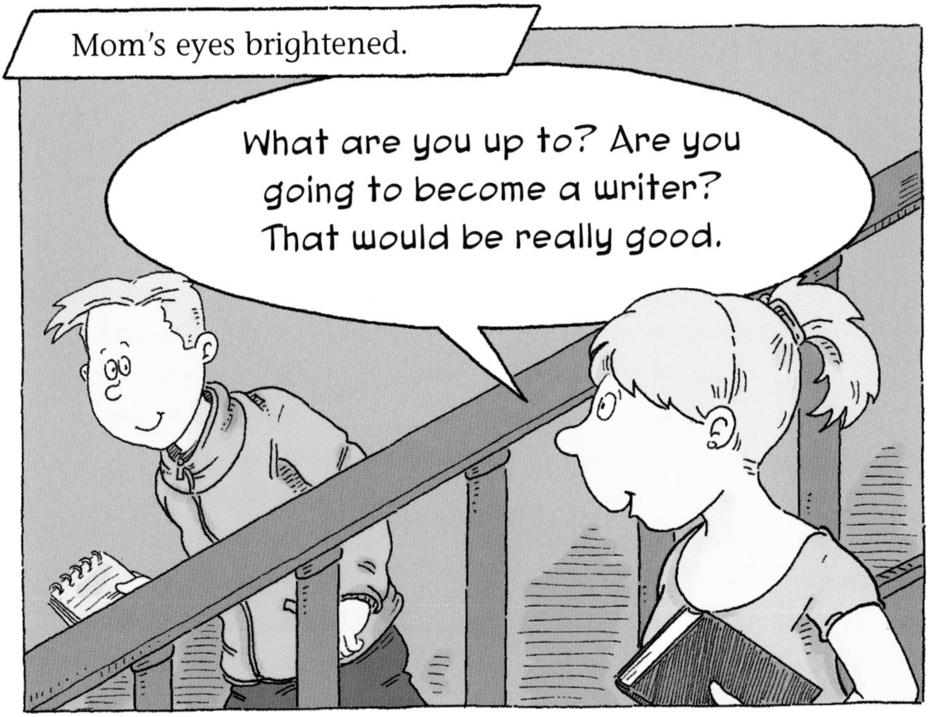
Mom's eyes brightened.
What are you up to? Are you going to become a writer? That would be really good.

"Maybe," Archie answered, eager to keep her happy.

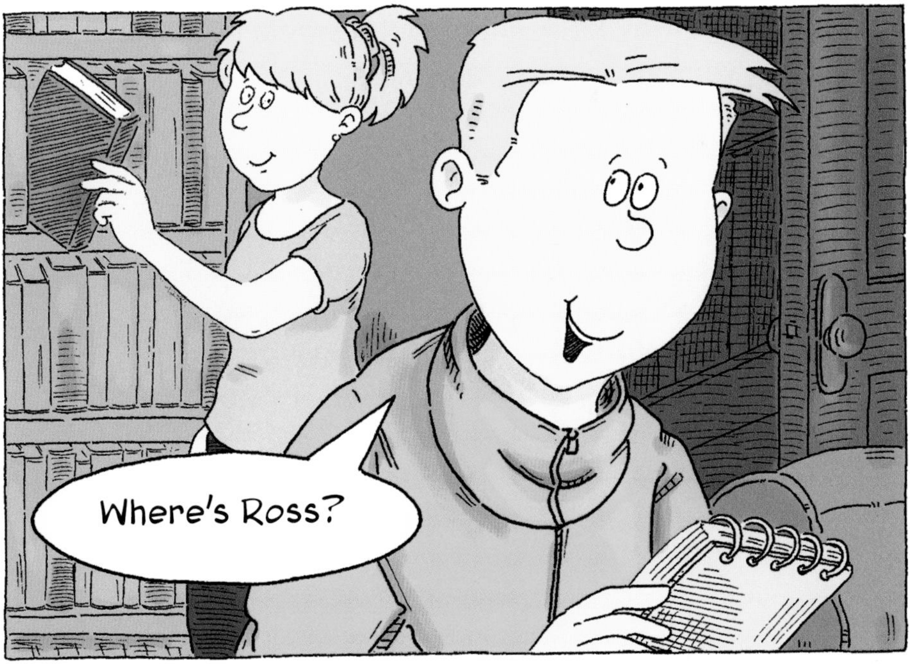
Where's Ross?

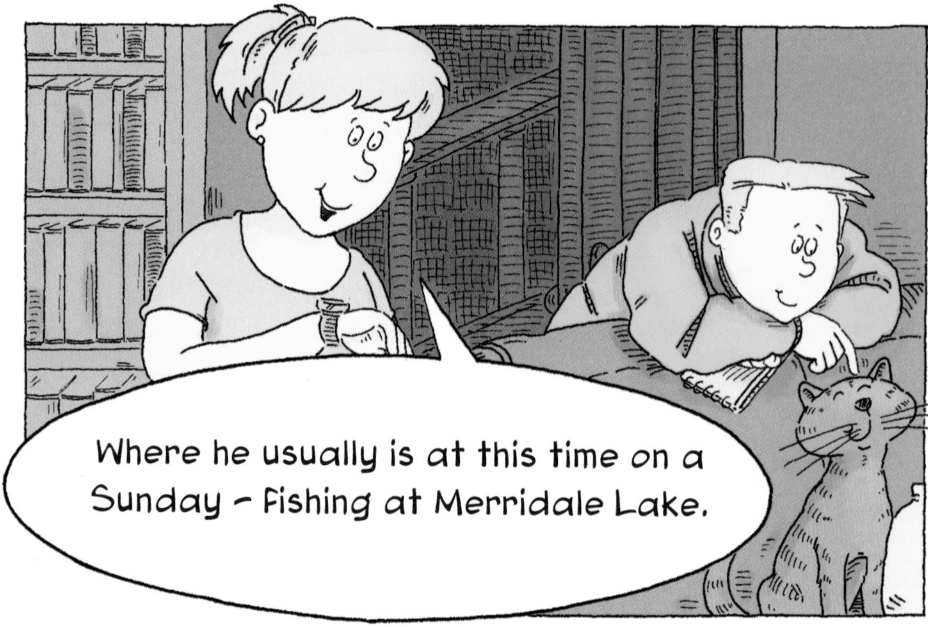
Where he usually is at this time on a Sunday - fishing at Merridale Lake.

“Thanks,” said Archie, leaving at his usual speed. Merridale Lake was at the bottom of the valley, and it wouldn’t take him long to get there. It would be a hard climb on the way back home, but it would be worth it if he got what he wanted from Ross.

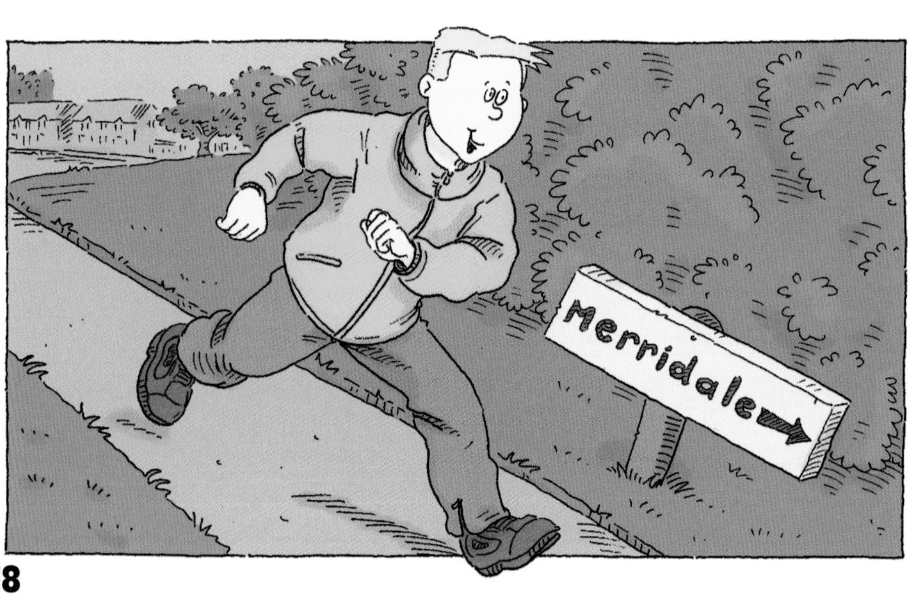
Merridale

CHAPTER THREE

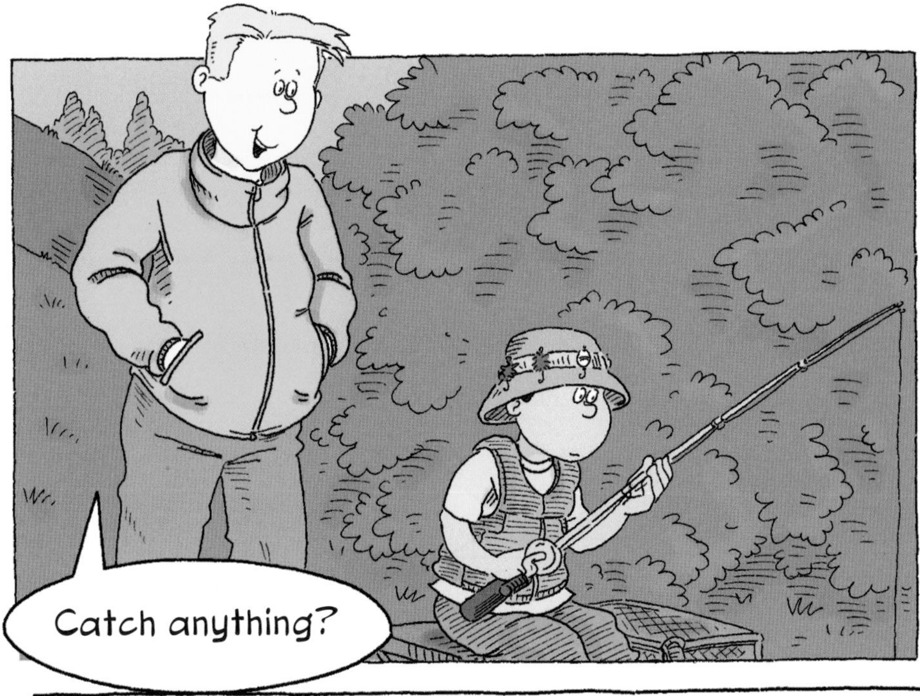
Catch anything?

Archie was very friendly when he saw his brother. Ross was the only person fishing on that part of the lake, but Archie knew Ross liked spending time alone.

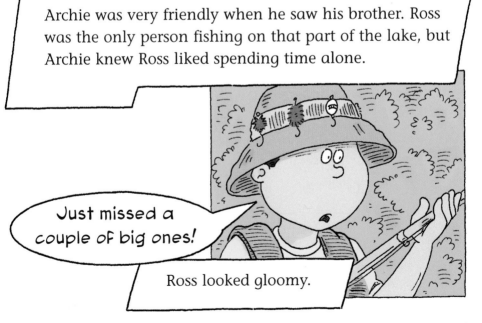

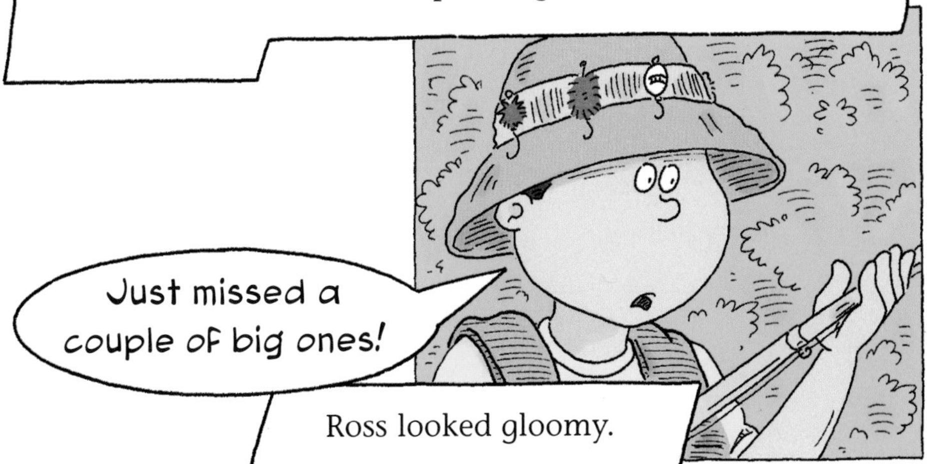
Just missed a couple of big ones!

Ross looked gloomy.

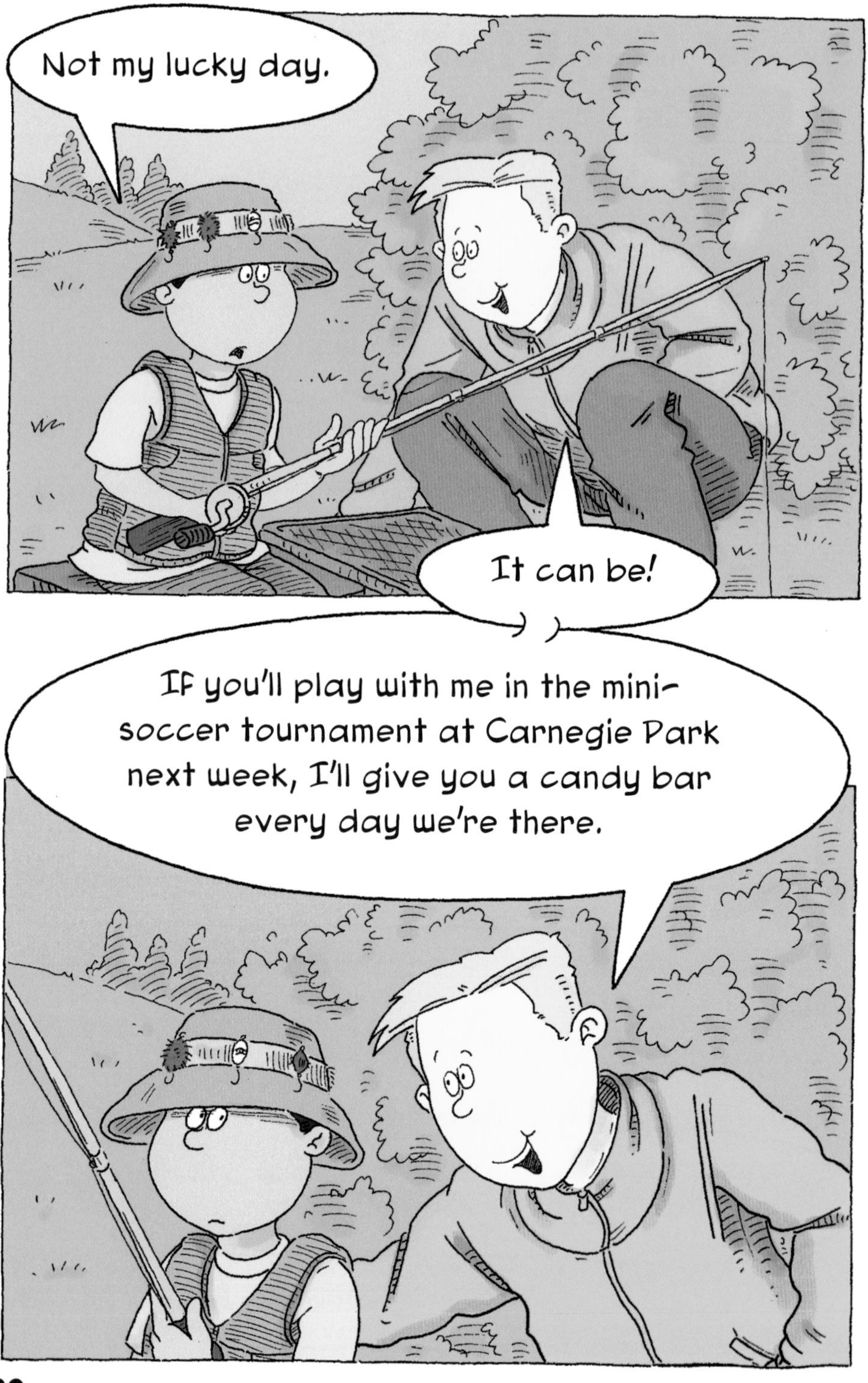
Not my lucky day.
It can be!
If you'll play with me in the mini-soccer tournament at Carnegie Park next week, I'll give you a candy bar every day we're there.

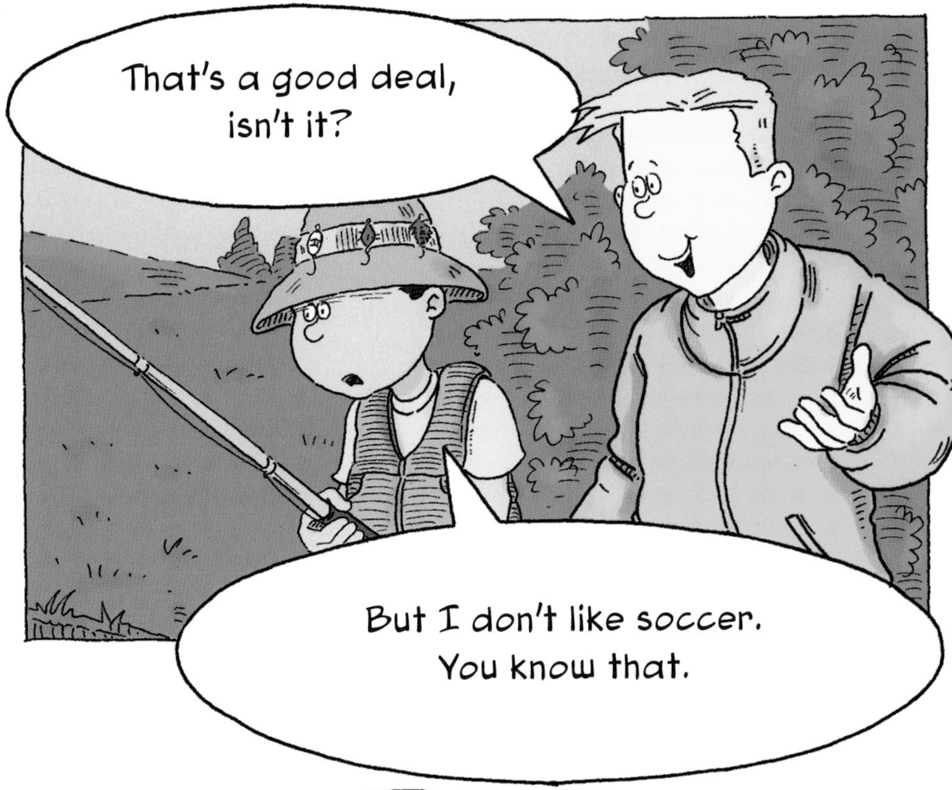
That's a good deal, isn't it?
But I don't like soccer. You know that.

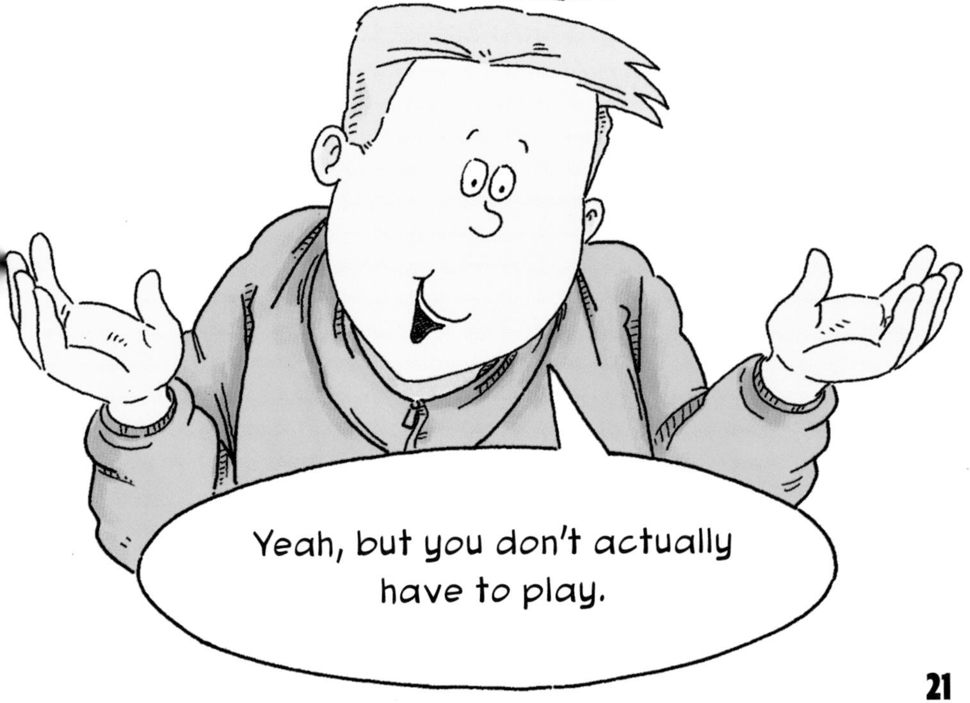
Yeah, but you don't actually have to play.

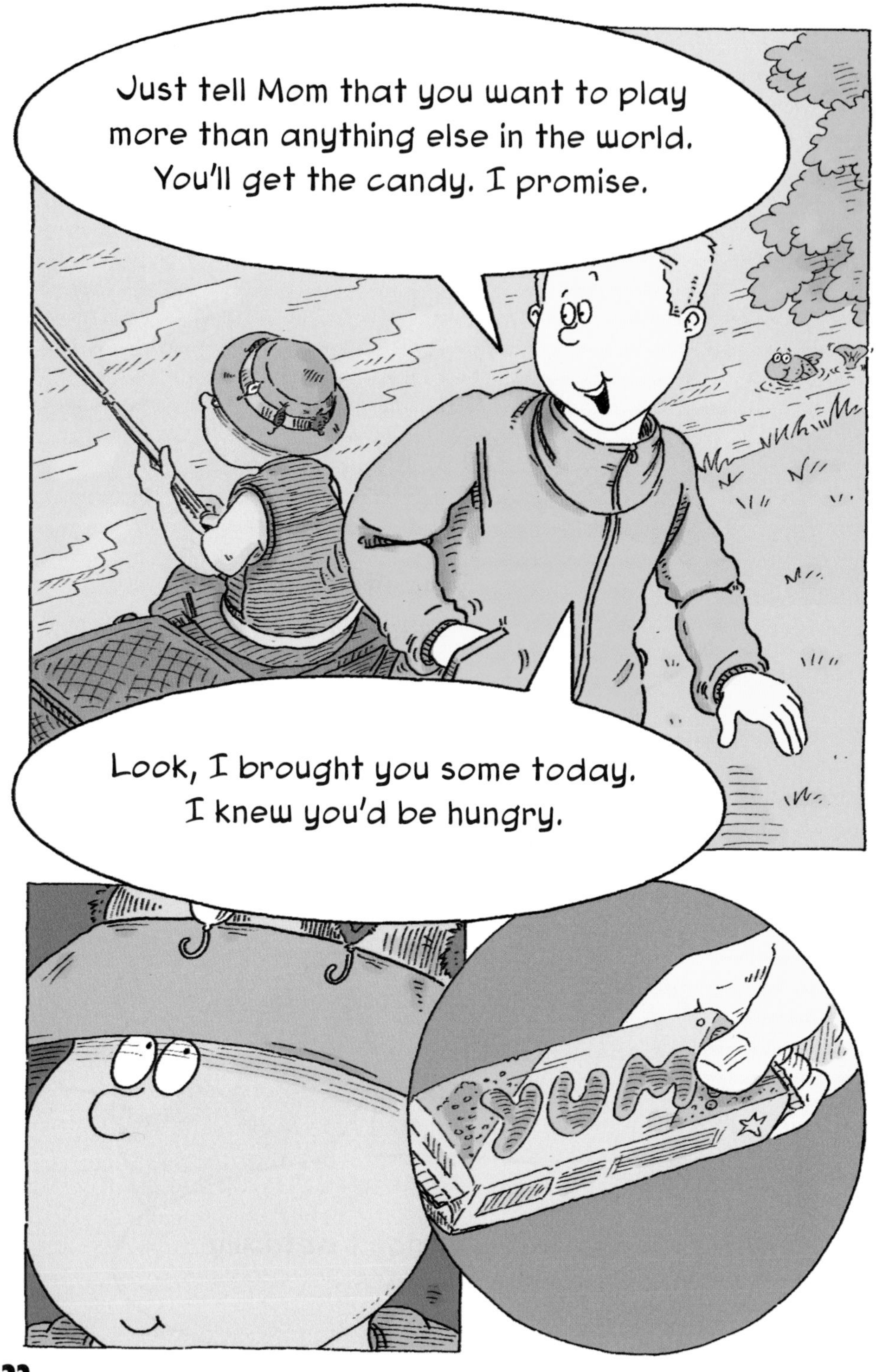
Just tell Mom that you want to play more than anything else in the world. You'll get the candy. I promise.
Look, I brought you some today. I knew you'd be hungry.
YUM!

Archie handed it over. Ross opened the candy bar immediately and stuffed half of it into his mouth. He didn't take his eyes off his fishing rod.

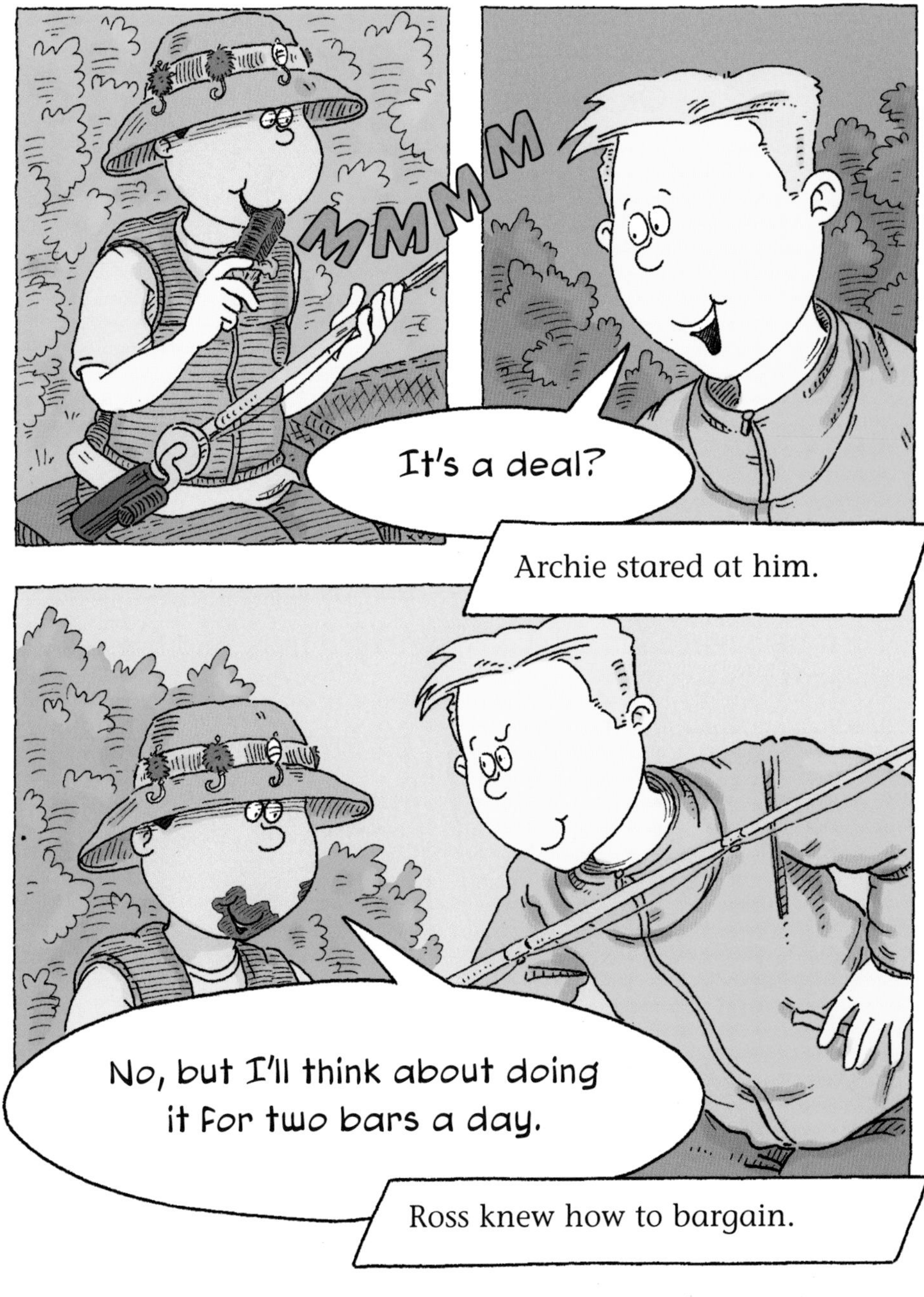
MMMMM
It's a deal?
Archie stared at him.
No, but I'll think about doing it for two bars a day.
Ross knew how to bargain.

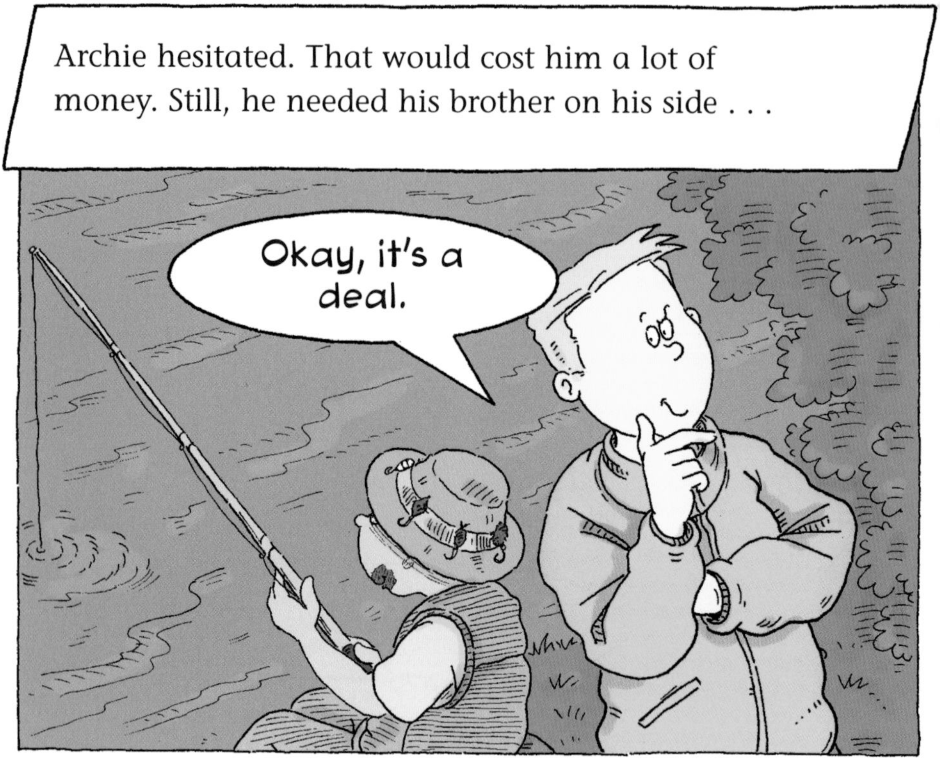
Archie hesitated. That would cost him a lot of money. Still, he needed his brother on his side . . .
Okay, it's a deal.

Then he opened his notebook, scribbled in it, and handed it over to Ross.

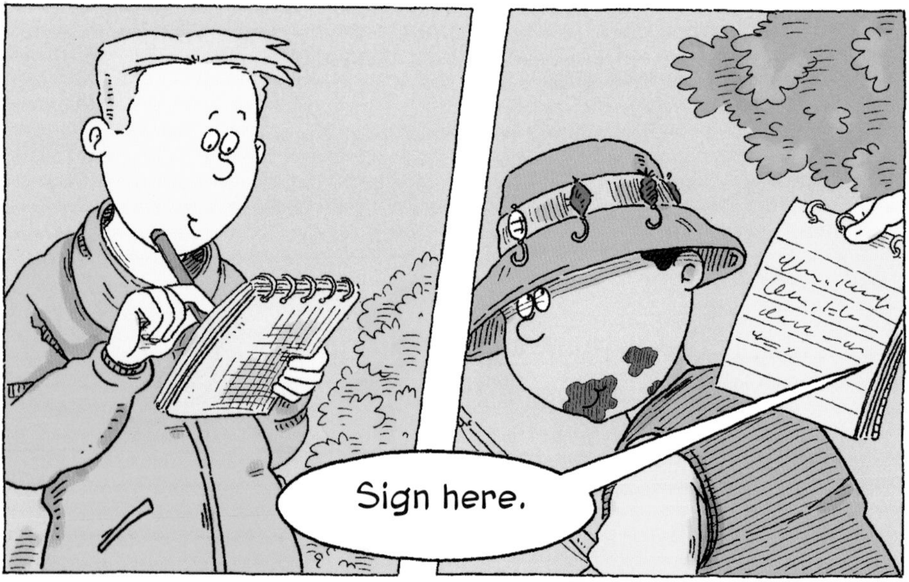
Sign here.

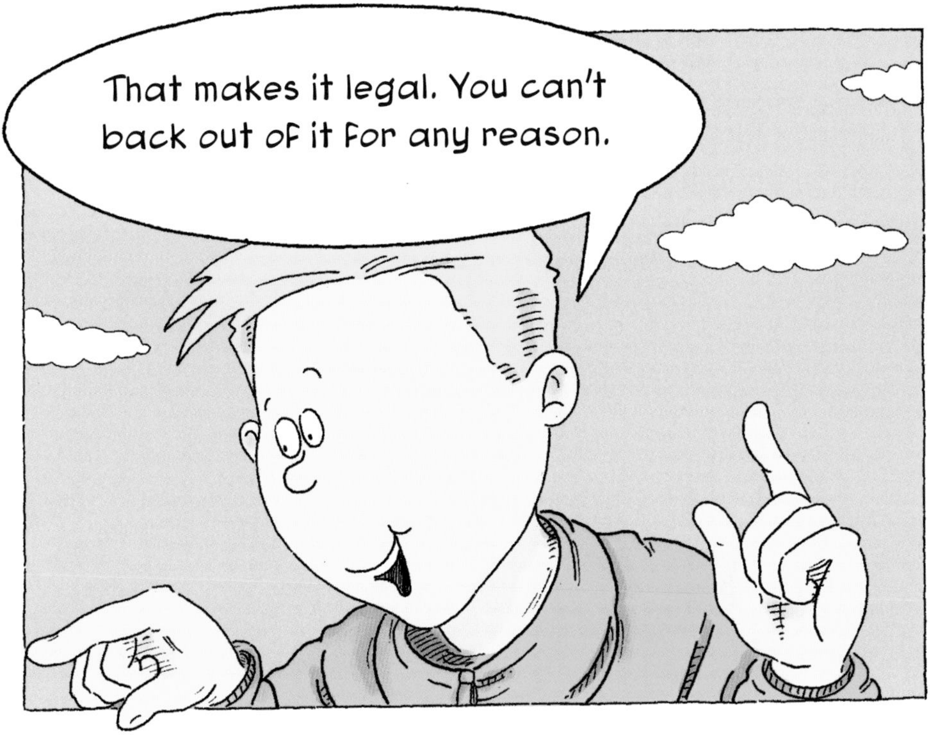
That makes it legal. You can't back out of it for any reason.

Ross tucked his fishing rod under his arm and awkwardly signed his name on the page. Archie grinned. He knew his brother couldn't resist chocolate.

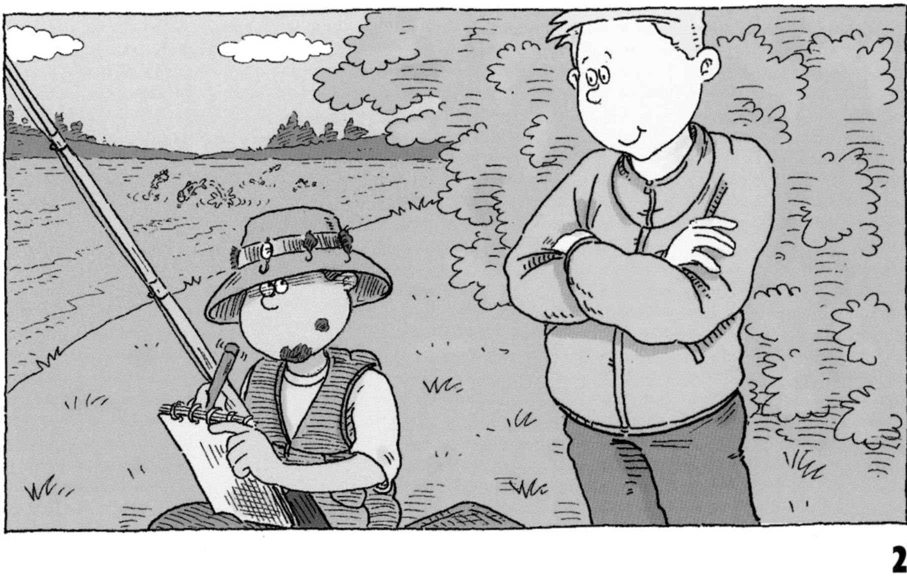

CHAPTER FOUR

Minutes later, Archie was puffing his way to the top of the hill, plotting how to get Jenny on his side.

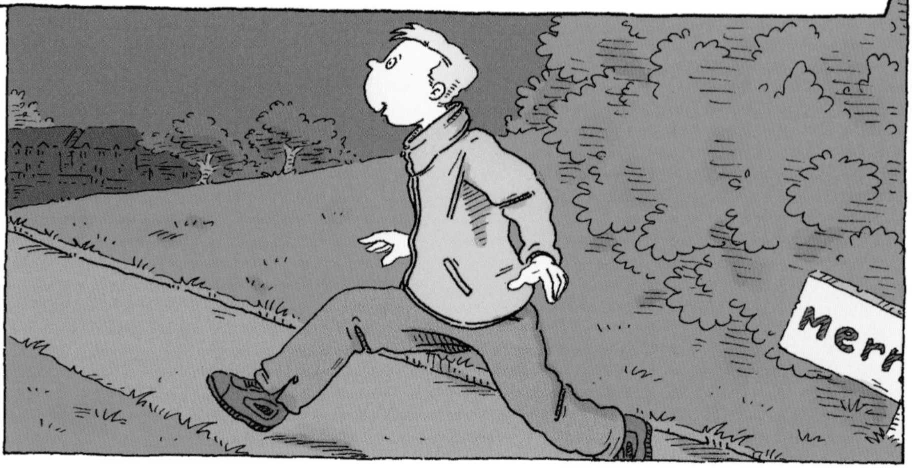
Merr

She liked soccer. She even practiced sometimes with Archie, but she loved tennis more. She was convinced she would win Wimbledon one day.

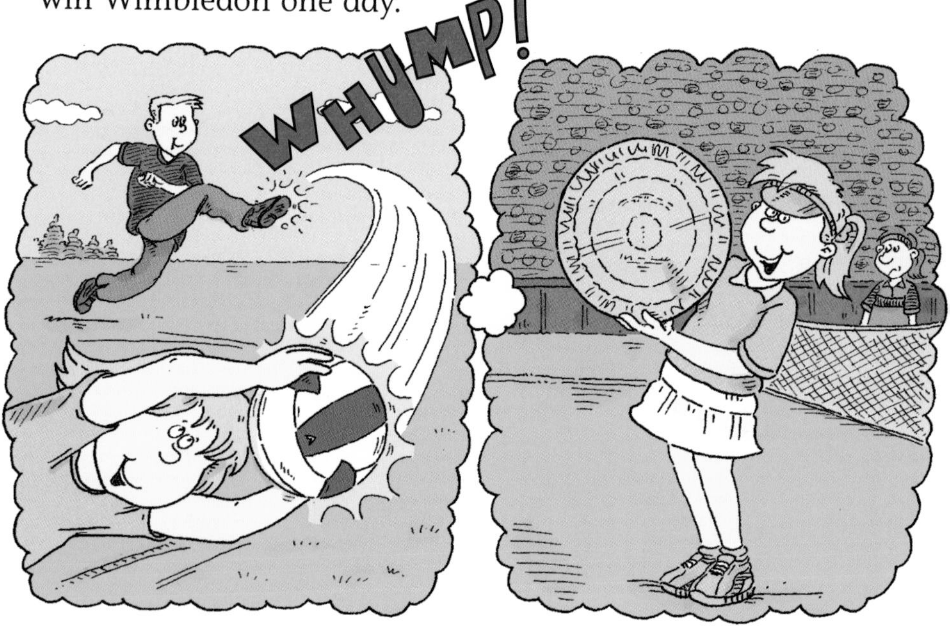
WHUMP!

Archie had to make sure Jenny would agree to play in the mini-soccer tournament as well as the tennis tournament. This would be tricky because Tom, a boy at her school who was also coming with his family to Carnegie Park, had agreed to be her tennis partner.

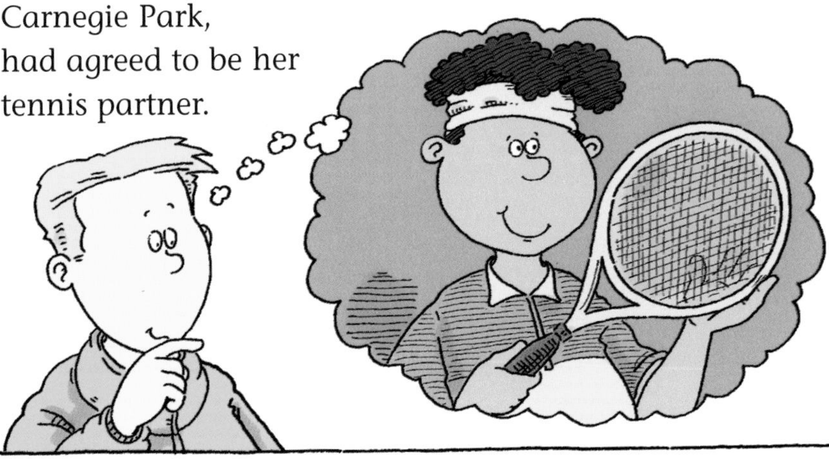

Archie crept into the house, trying not to disturb his mom. He went up to his room, so he could work out a plan in peace.

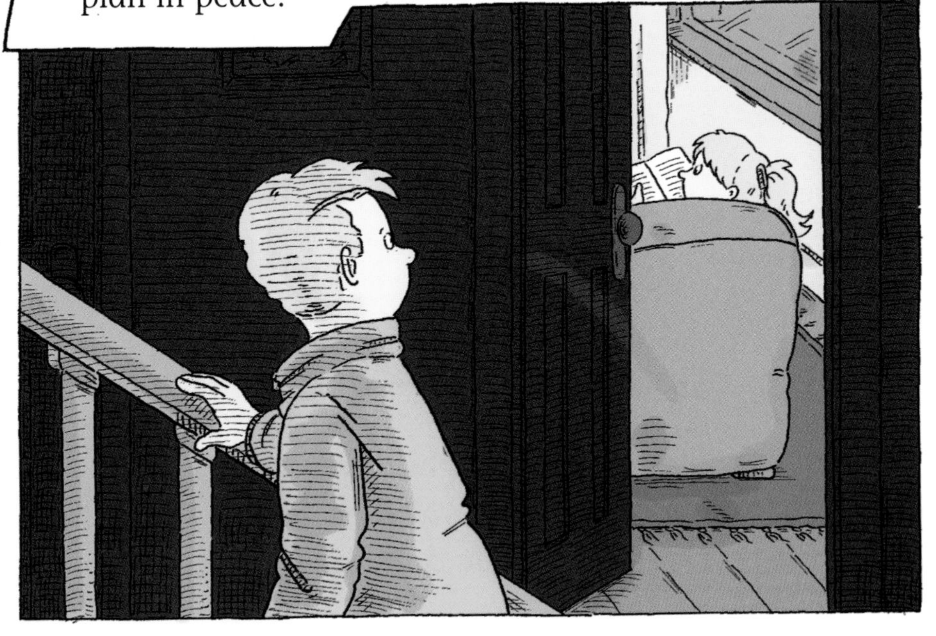

After lunch Archie took his notebook and set off on his bike. Tom would be practicing with Jenny. First, he had to win them over by playing some tennis.

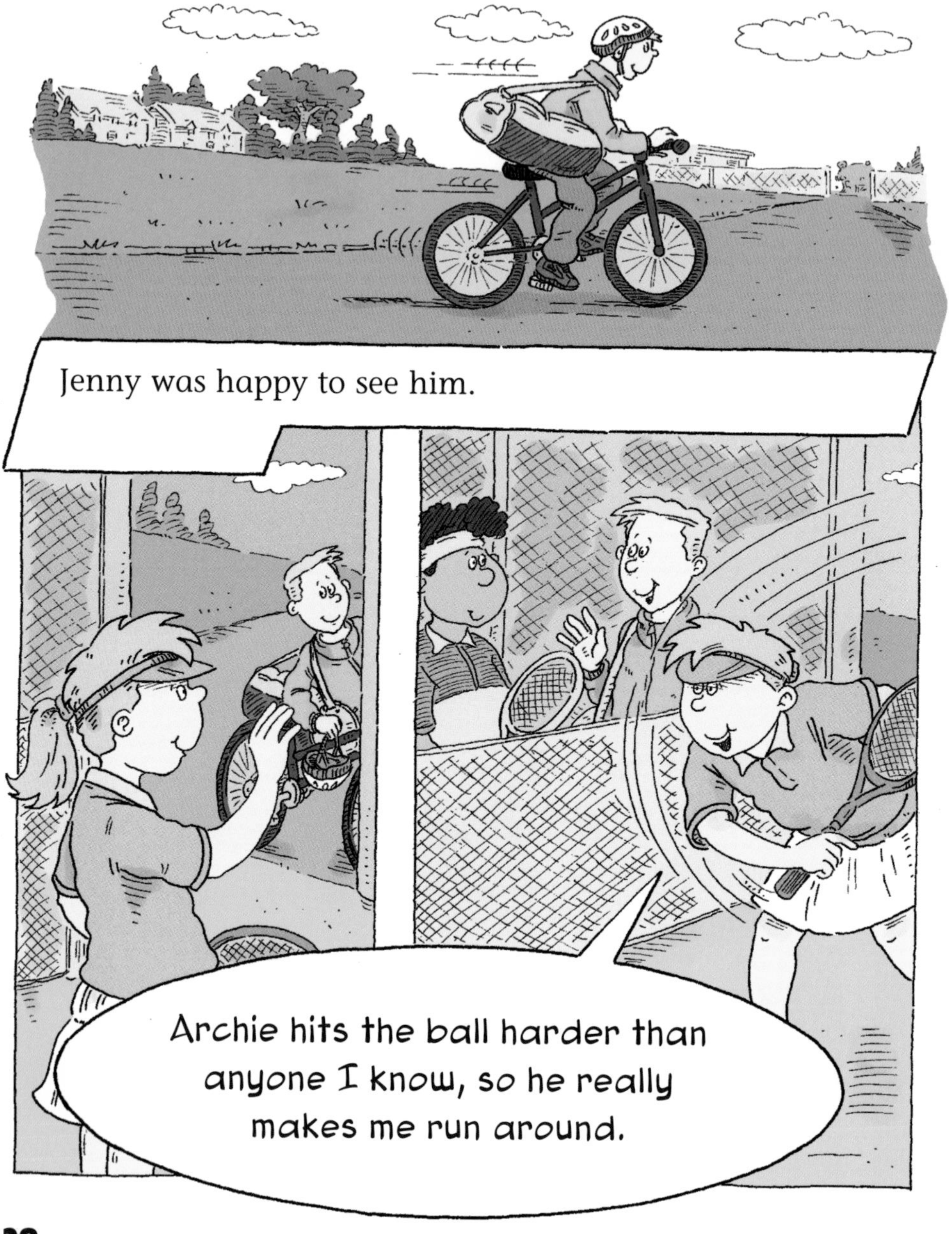
Jenny was happy to see him.
Archie hits the ball harder than anyone I know, so he really makes me run around.

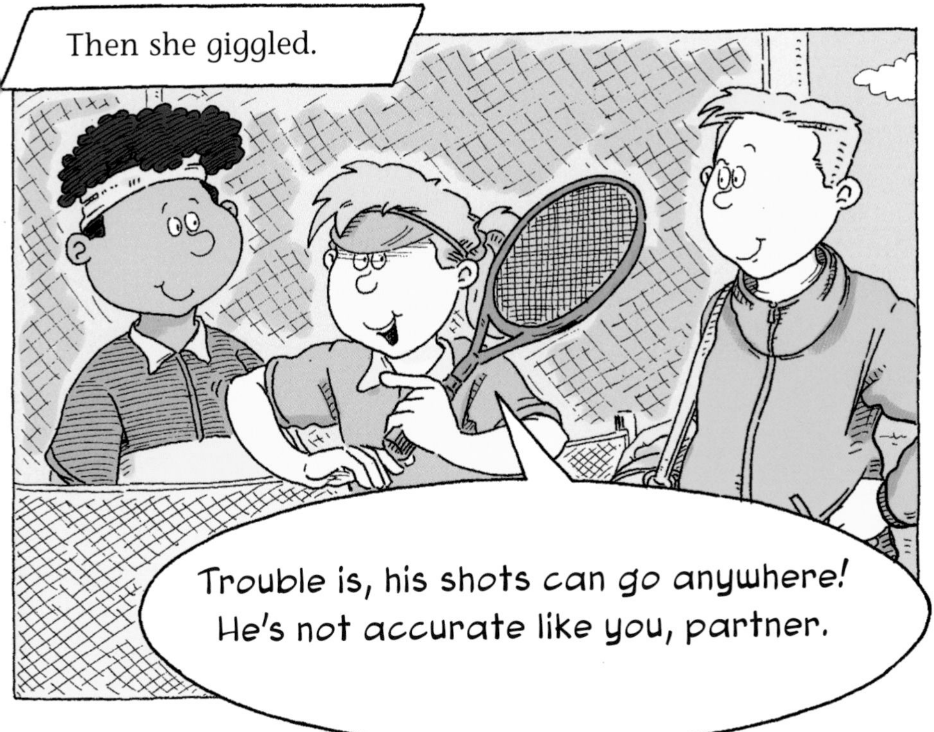
Then she giggled.
Trouble is, his shots can go anywhere! He's not accurate like you, partner.

Archie didn't contradict her, but when they were playing, he tried to avoid making any wild shots. For his plan to work, he needed them both to believe that he was really improving as a tennis player.

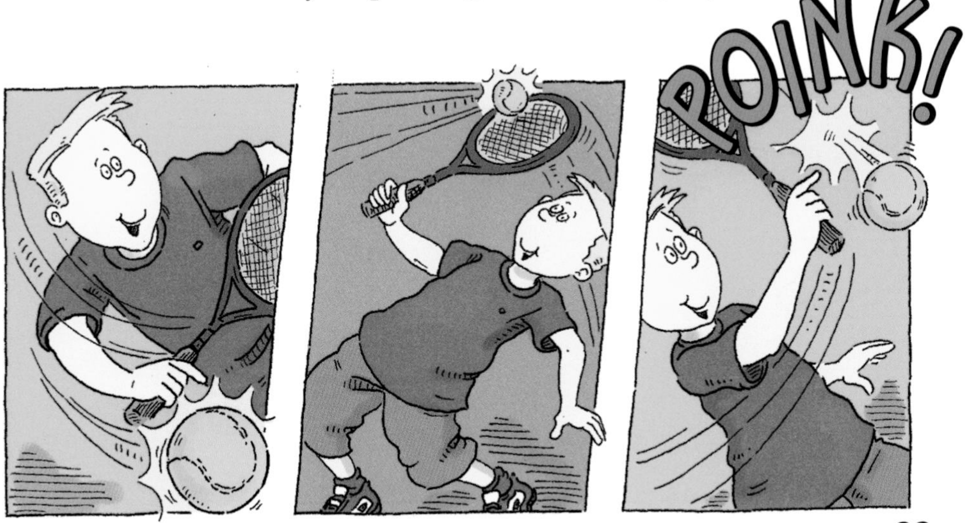
POINK!

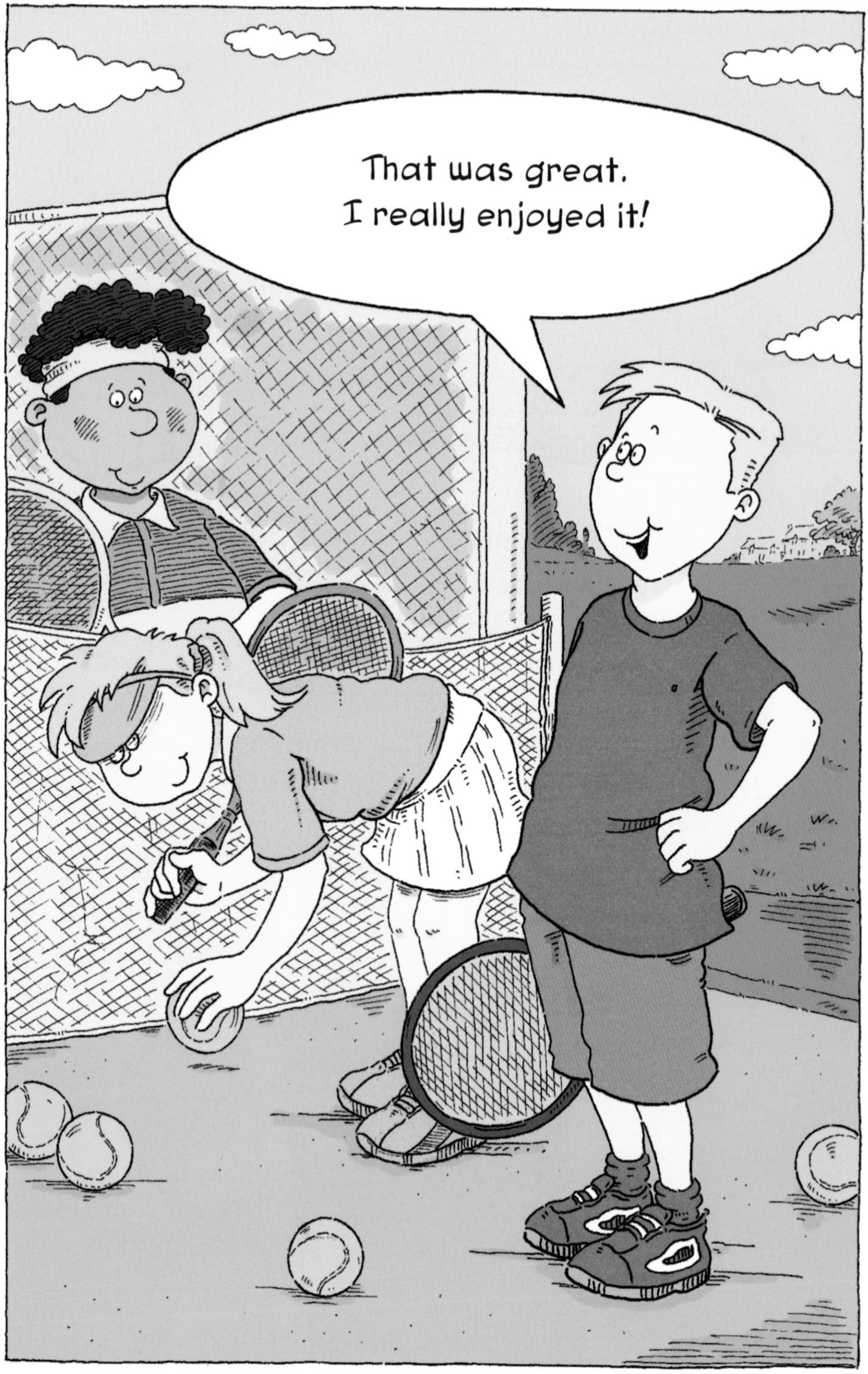
That was great.
I really enjoyed it!

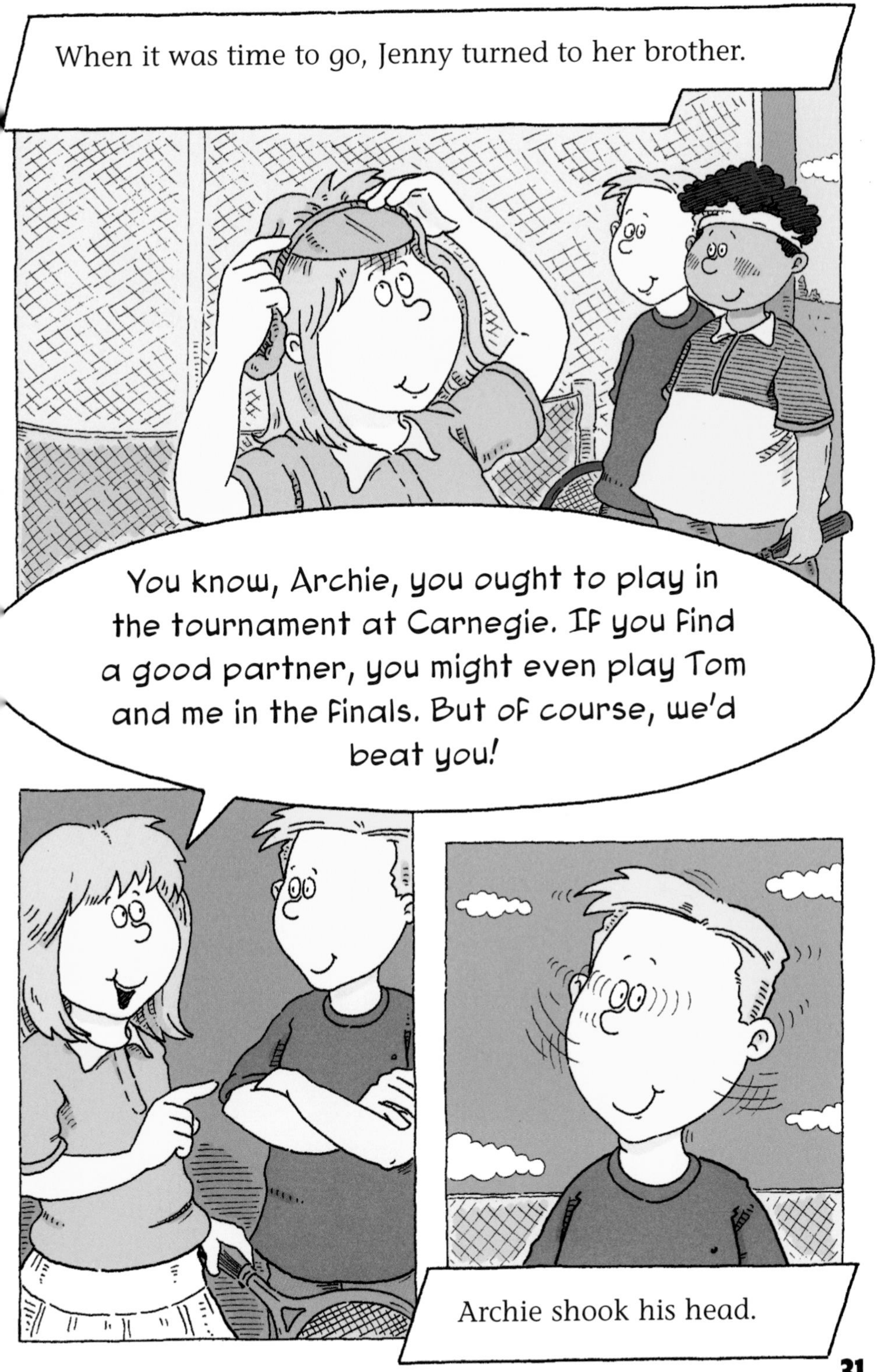
When it was time to go, Jenny turned to her brother.
You know, Archie, you ought to play in the tournament at Carnegie. If you find a good partner, you might even play Tom and me in the finals. But of course, we'd beat you!
Archie shook his head.

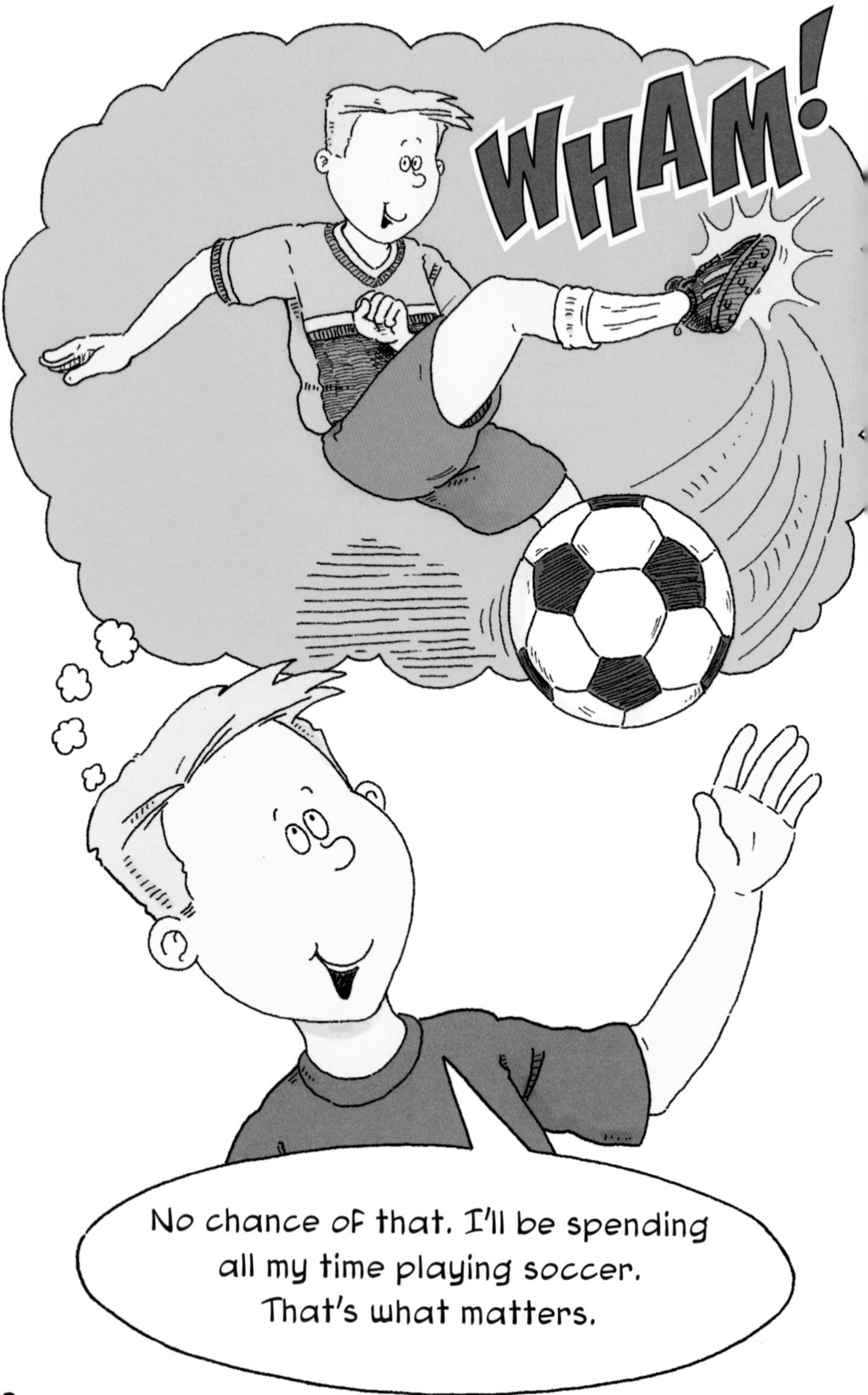
WHAM!
No chance of that. I'll be spending all my time playing soccer. That's what matters.

Once he and Tom were in the boys' locker room, however, he put his plan into action.

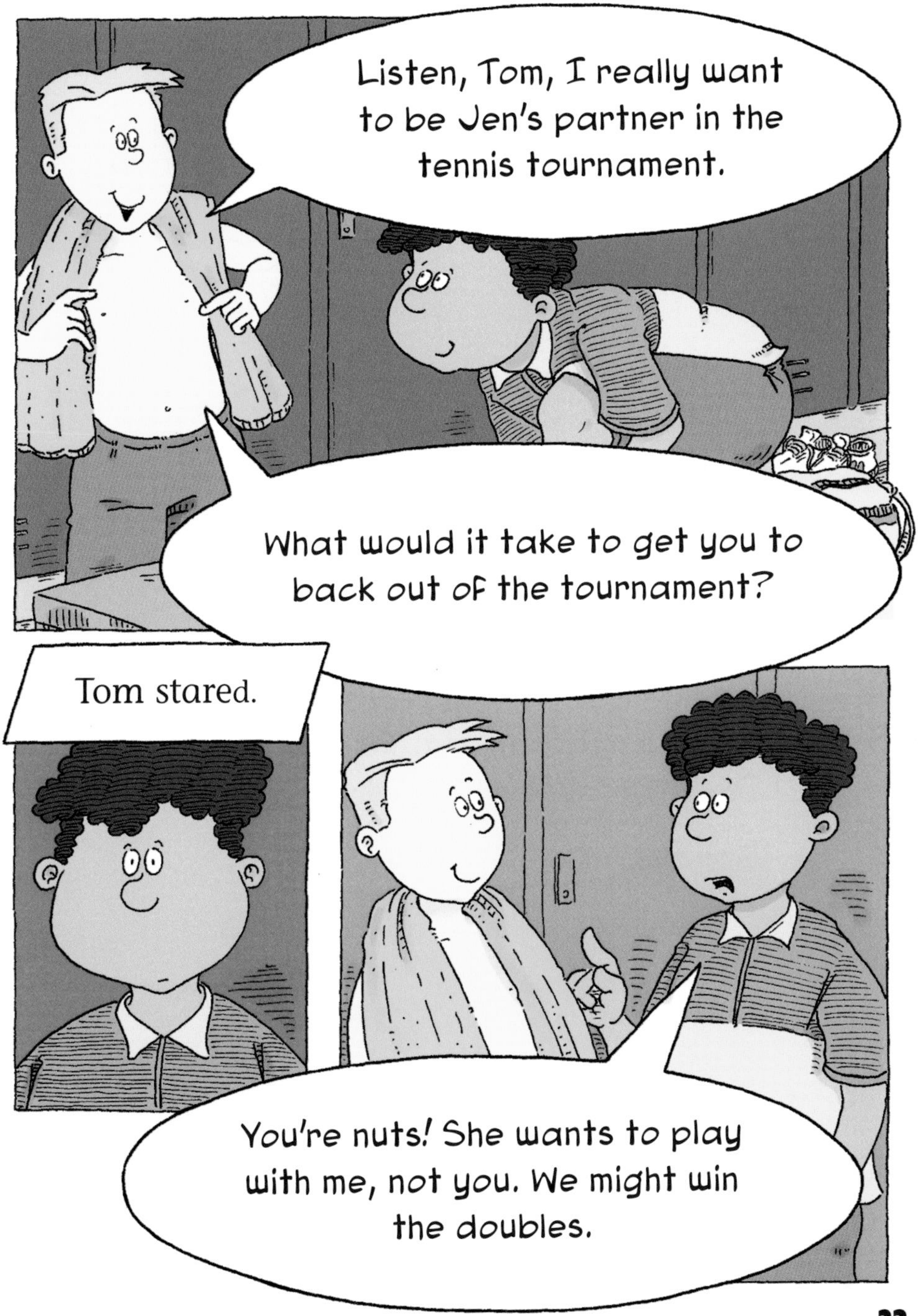
Listen, Tom, I really want to be Jen's partner in the tennis tournament.
What would it take to get you to back out of the tournament?
Tom stared.
You're nuts! She wants to play with me, not you. We might win the doubles.

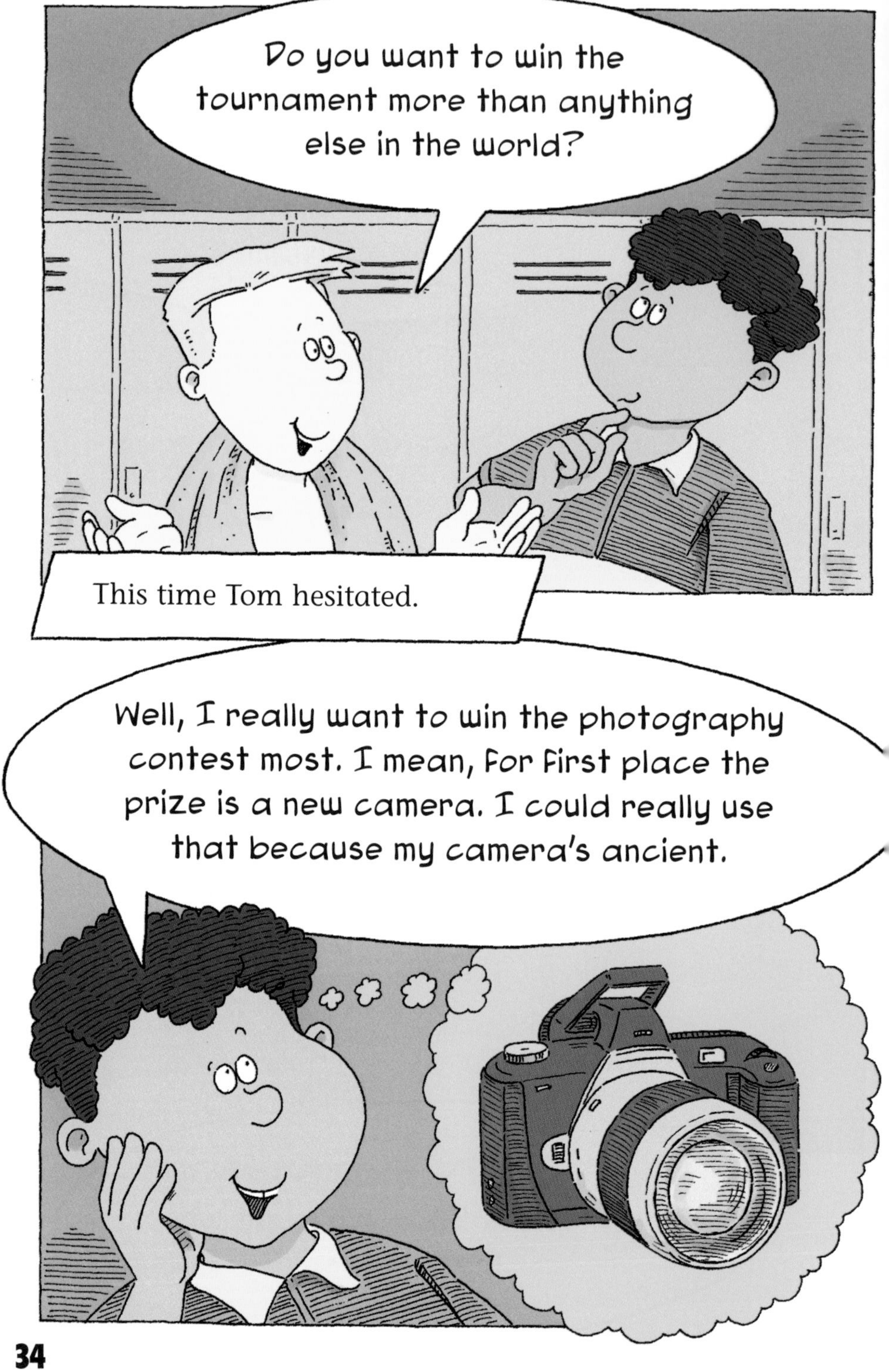
Do you want to win the tournament more than anything else in the world?
This time Tom hesitated.
Well, I really want to win the photography contest most. I mean, for first place the prize is a new camera. I could really use that because my camera's ancient.

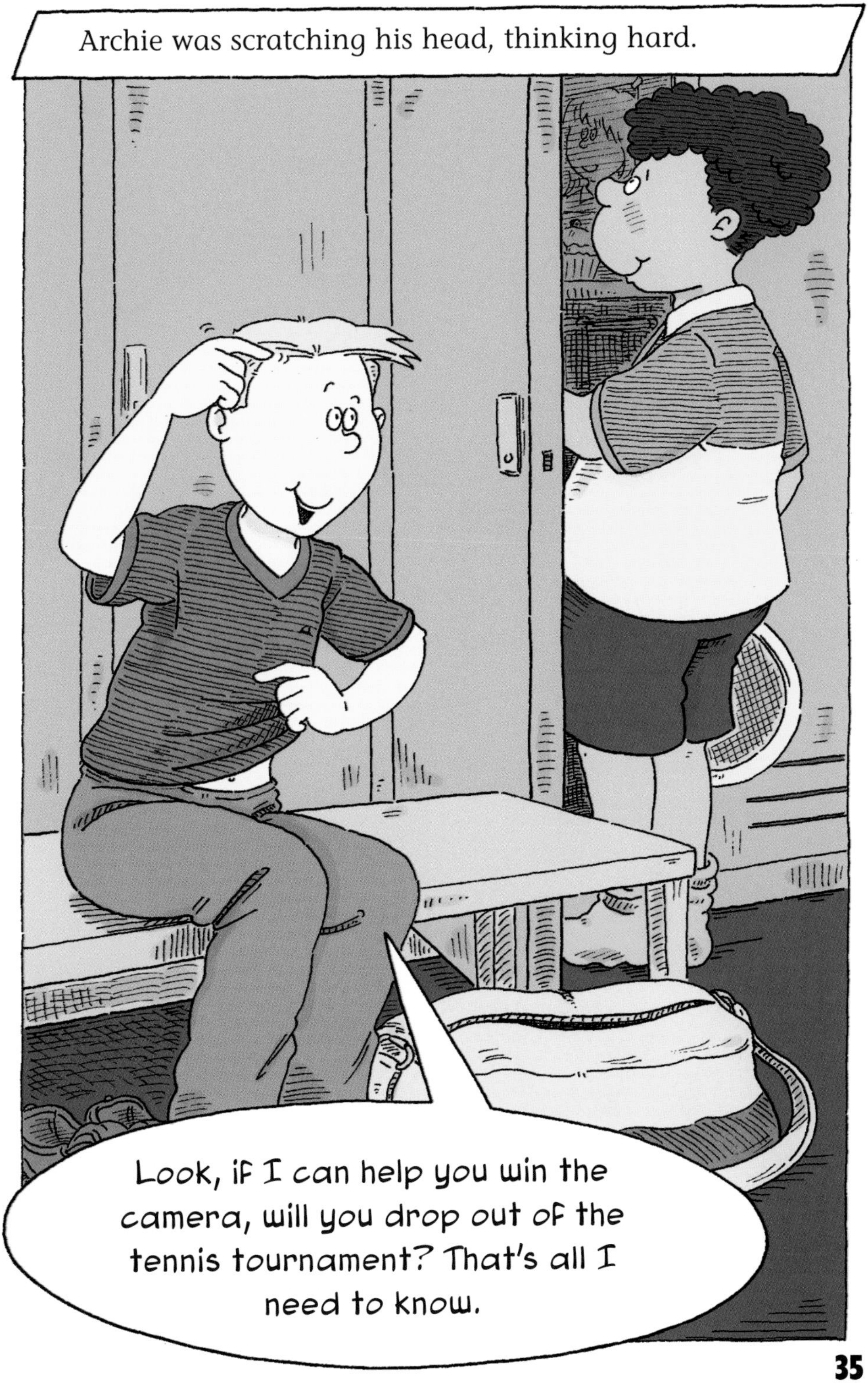
Archie was scratching his head, thinking hard.
Look, if I can help you win the camera, will you drop out of the tennis tournament? That's all I need to know.

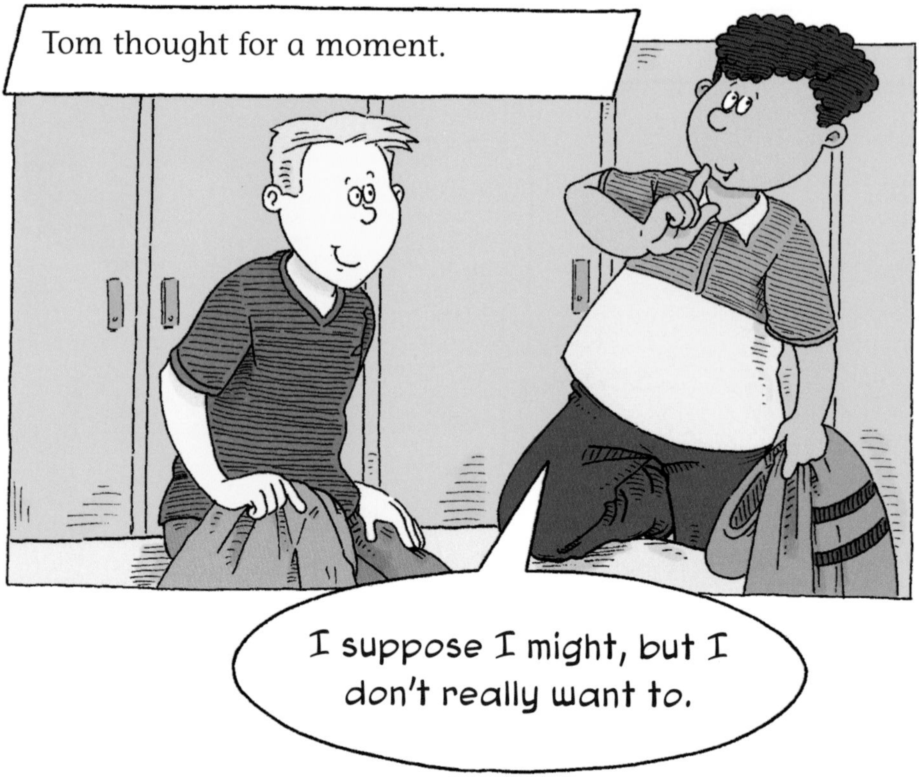
Tom thought for a moment.
I suppose I might, but I don't really want to.

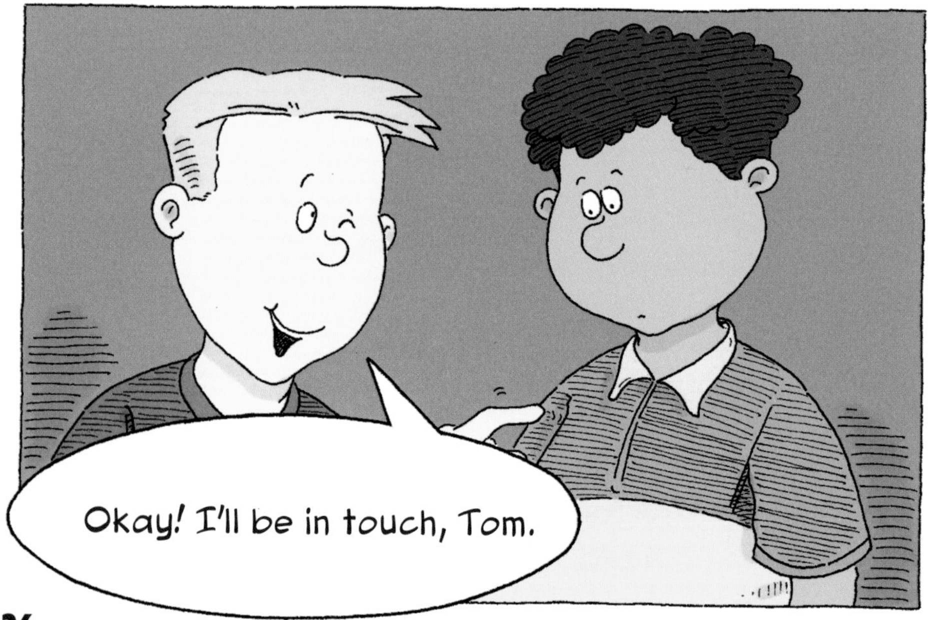
Okay! I'll be in touch, Tom.

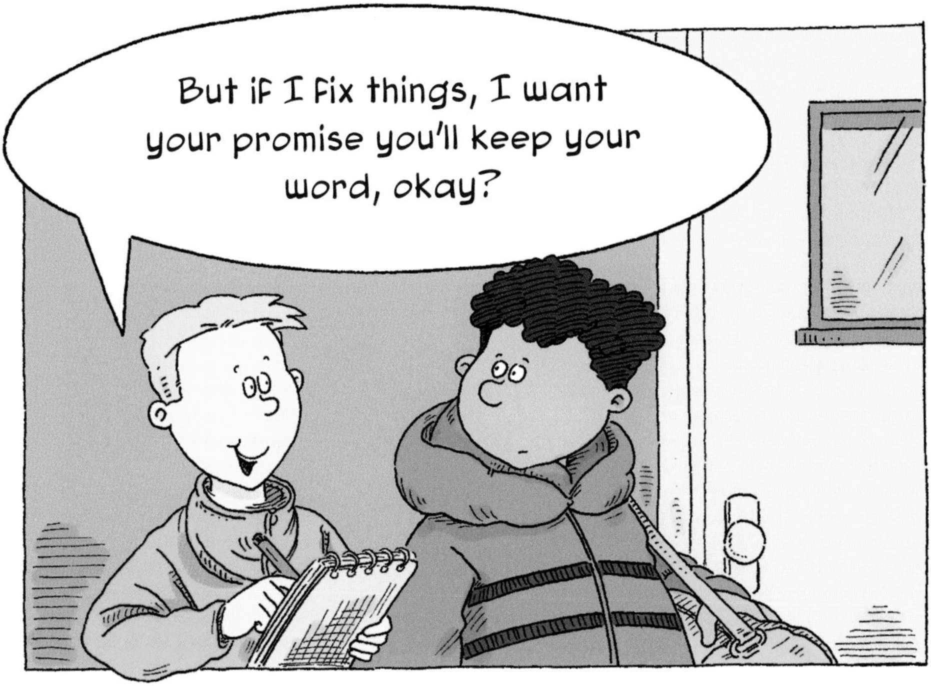
But if I fix things, I want your promise you'll keep your word, okay?

Tom gave a nod as Archie slid his notebook back into his pocket before walking toward his bike. This wasn't the time to talk to his sister about anything.

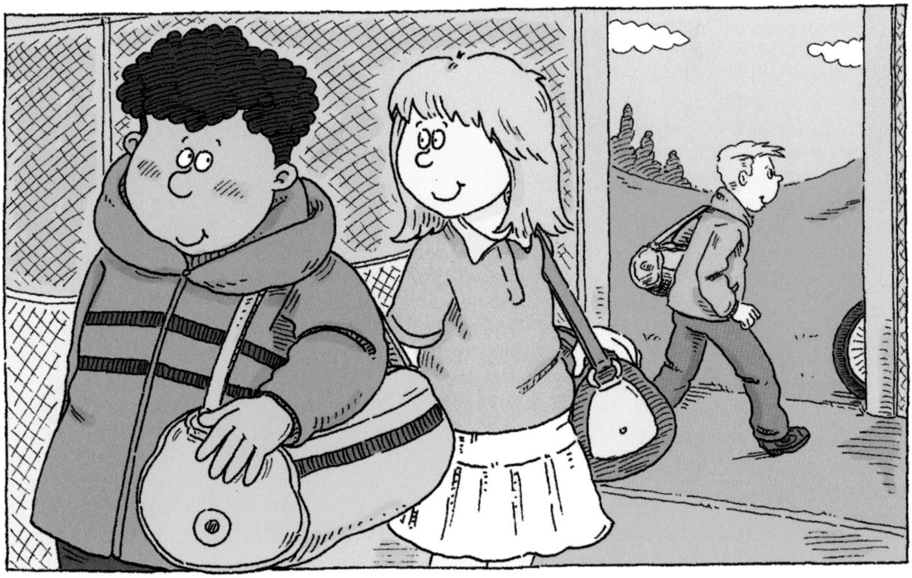

CHAPTER FIVE

The night before they went on vacation, Archie biked over to Kyle's house and suggested they practice soccer.

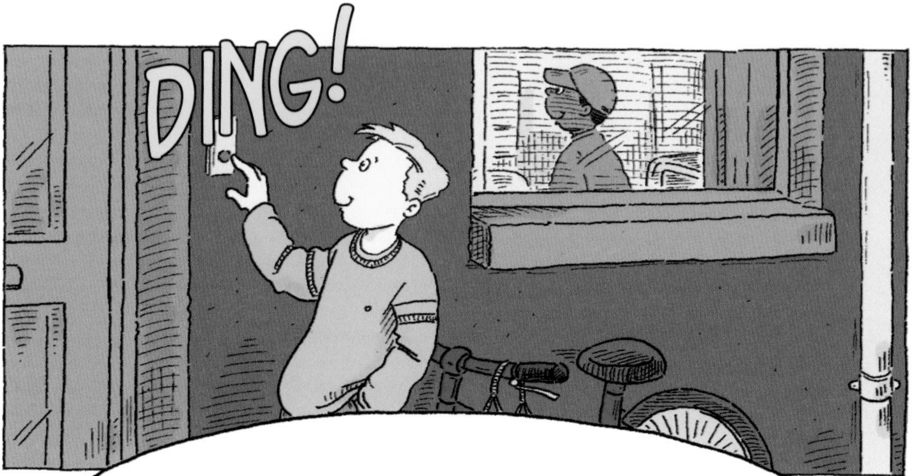
DING!

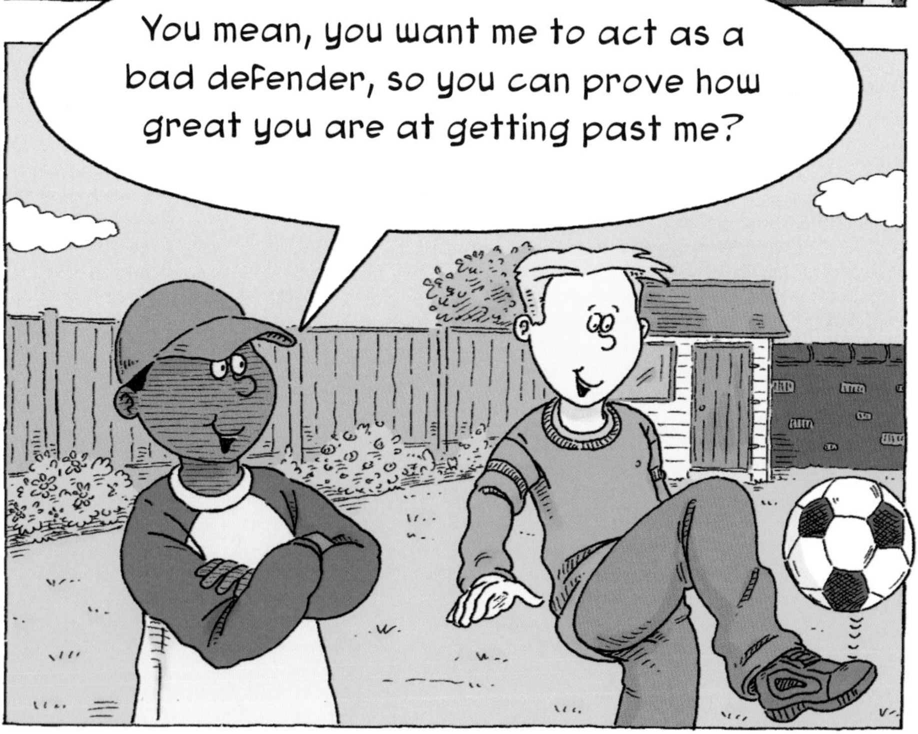
You mean, you want me to act as a bad defender, so you can prove how great you are at getting past me?

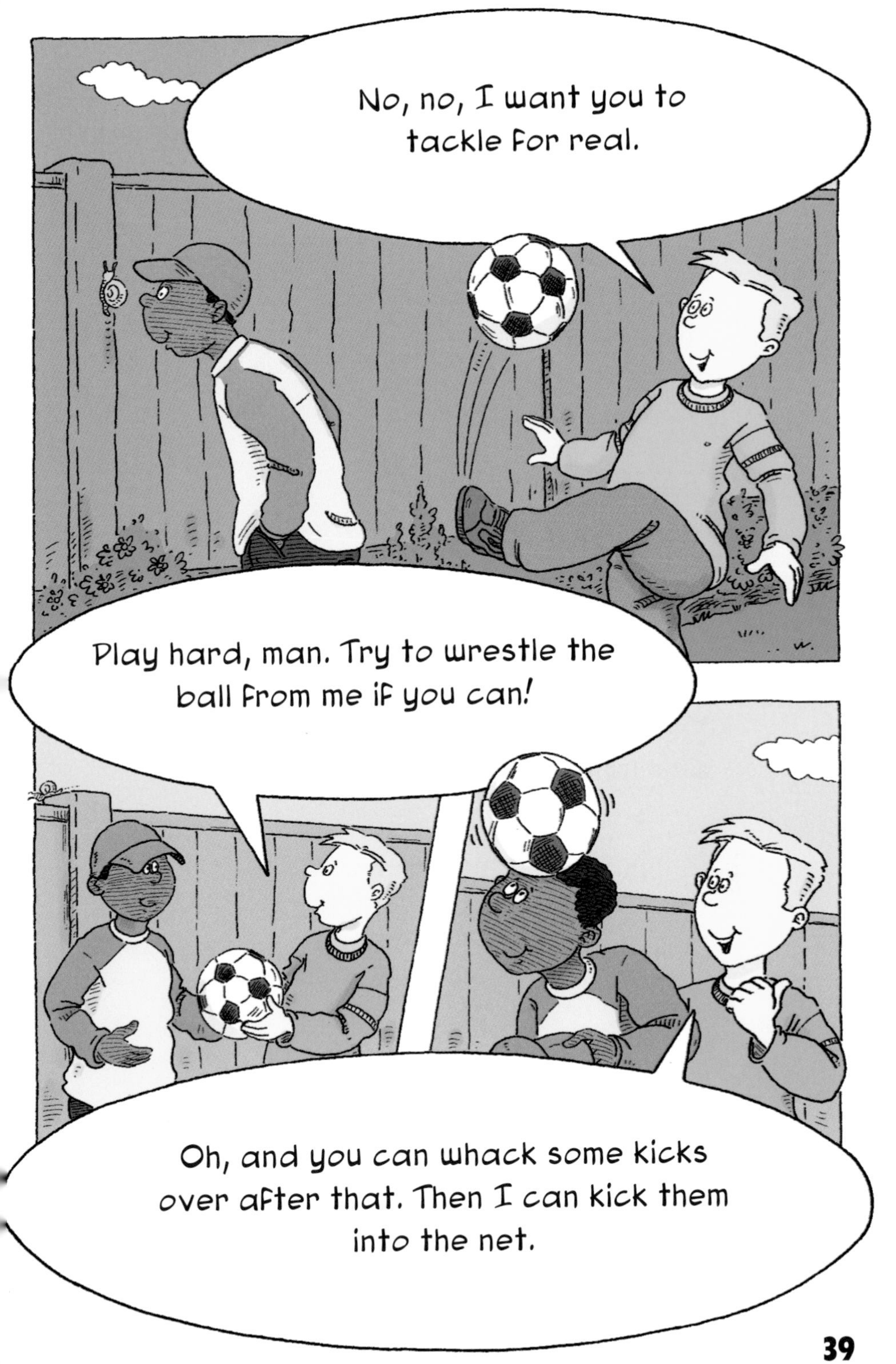
No, no, I want you to tackle for real.
Play hard, man. Try to wrestle the ball from me if you can!
Oh, and you can whack some kicks over after that. Then I can kick them into the net.

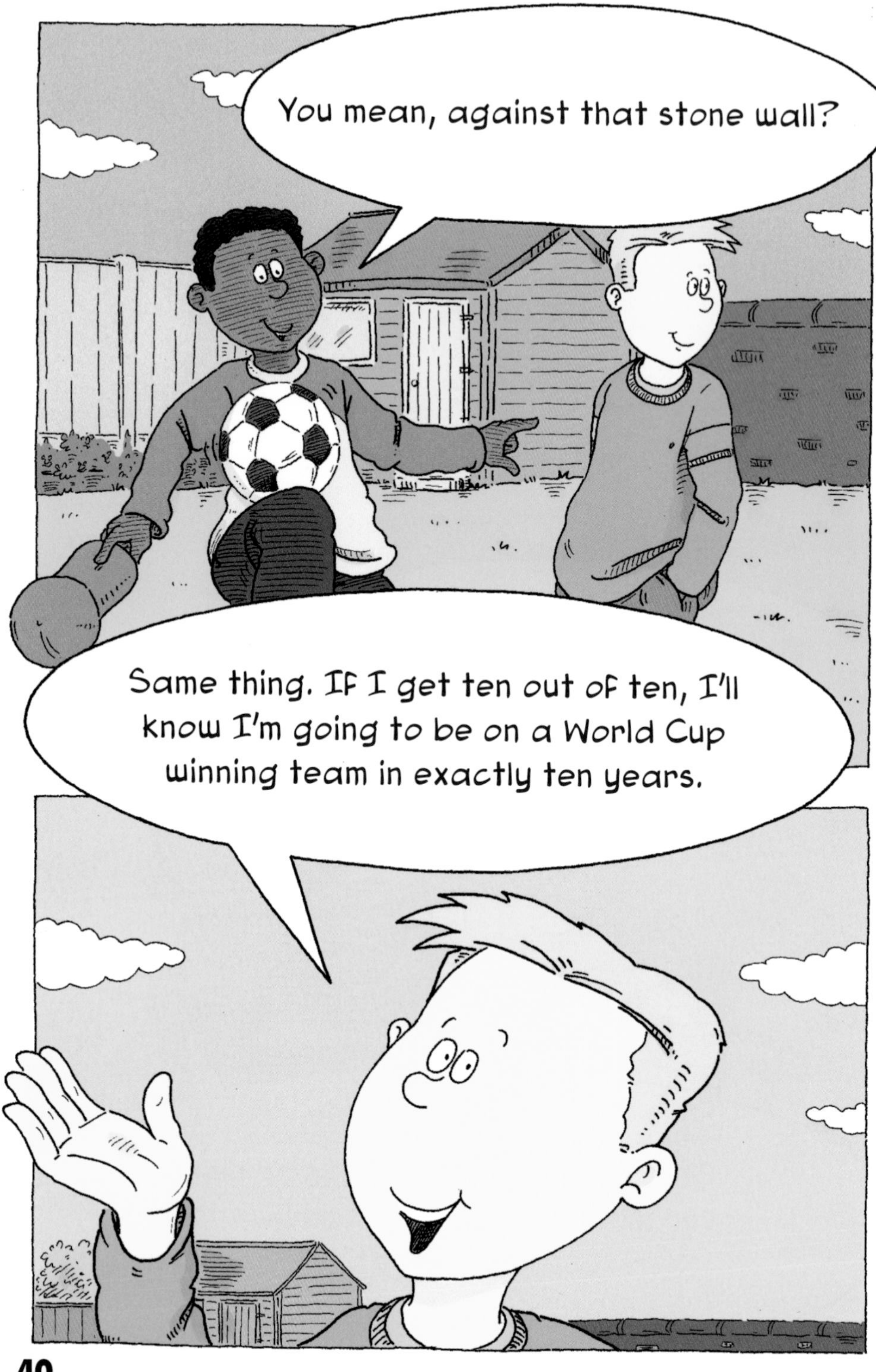

You mean, against that stone wall?
Same thing. If I get ten out of ten, I'll know I'm going to be on a World Cup winning team in exactly ten years.

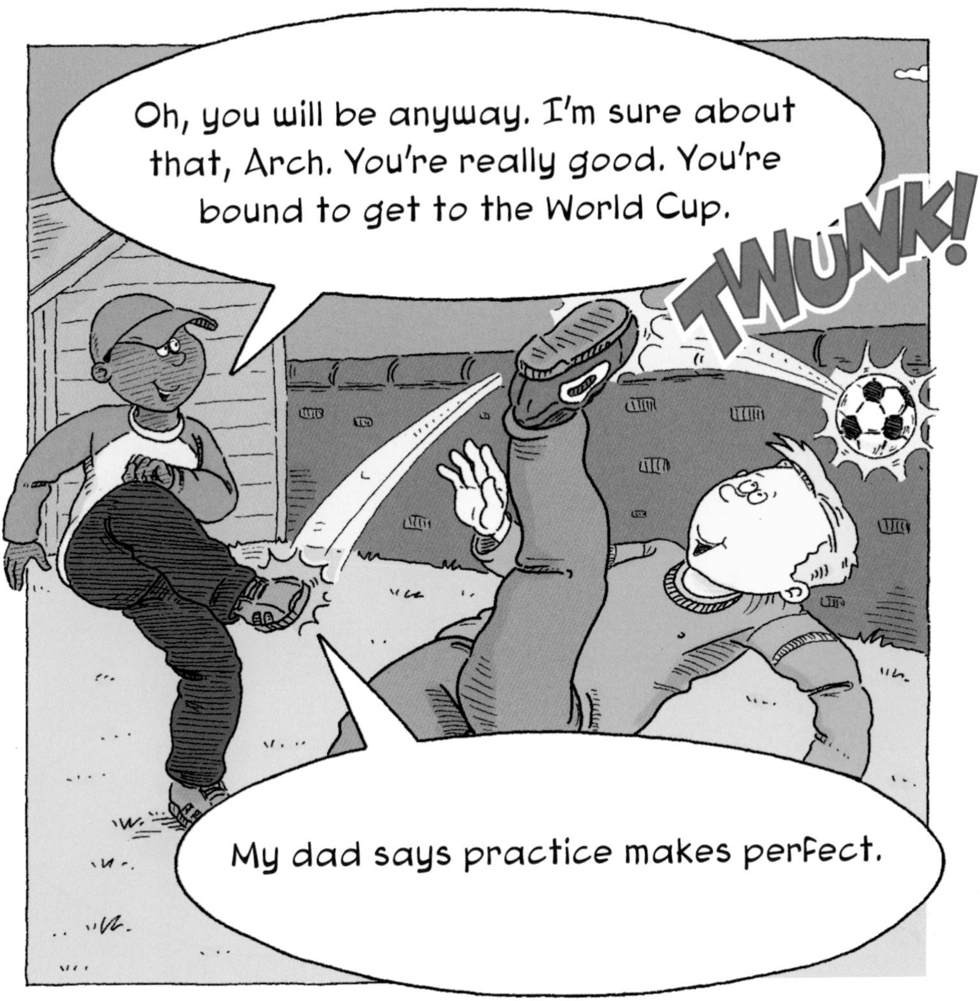
Oh, you will be anyway. I'm sure about that, Arch. You're really good. You're bound to get to the World Cup.
TWUNK!
My dad says practice makes perfect.

It was only when the practice was over that Archie finally asked Kyle an important question.

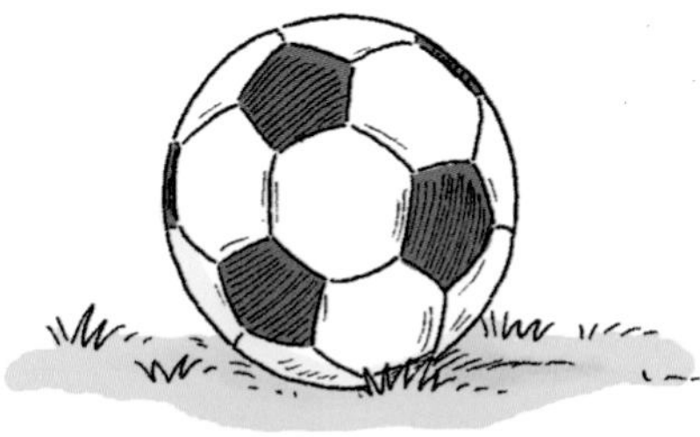

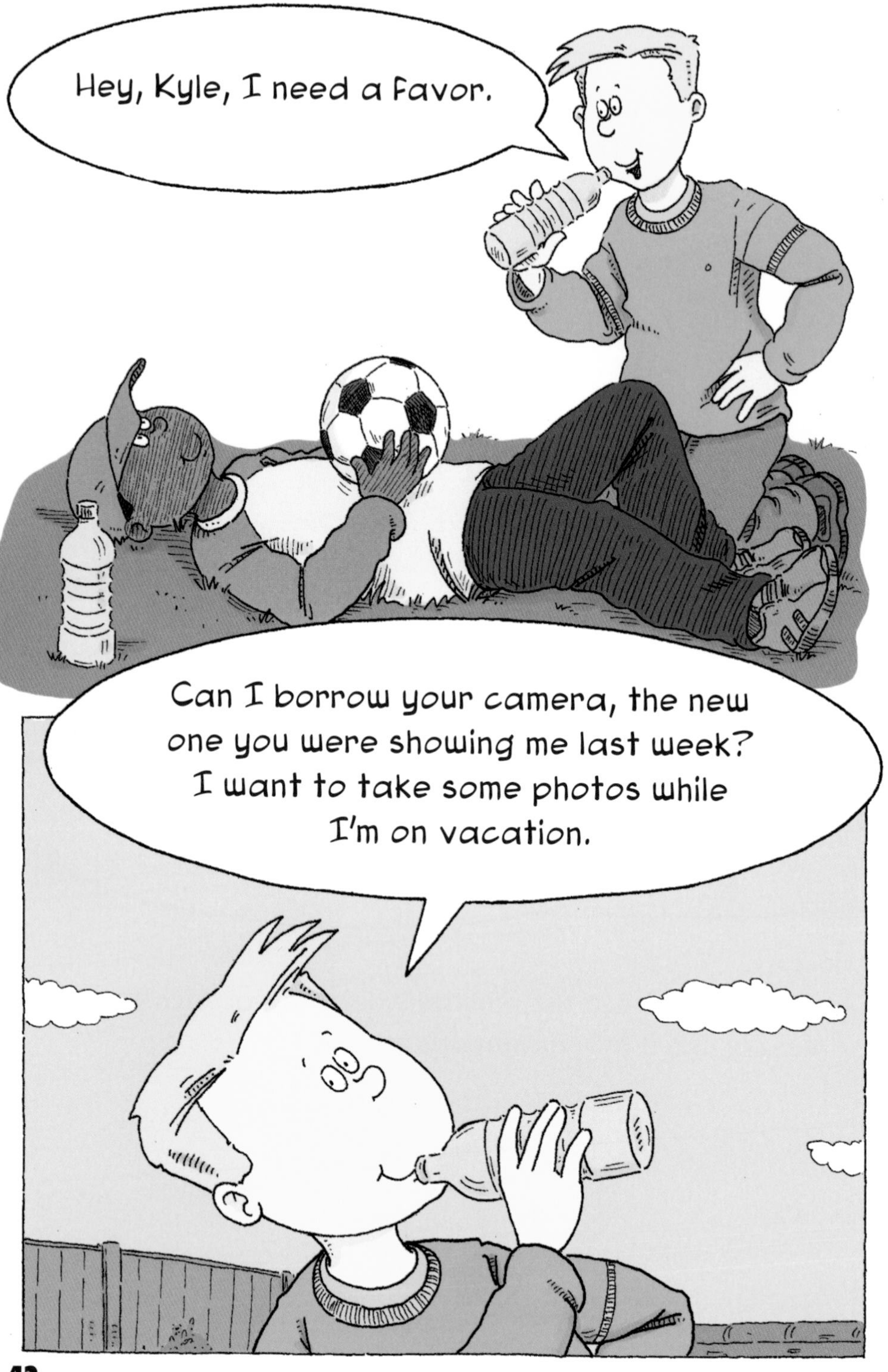
Hey, Kyle, I need a favor.
Can I borrow your camera, the new one you were showing me last week? I want to take some photos while I'm on vacation.

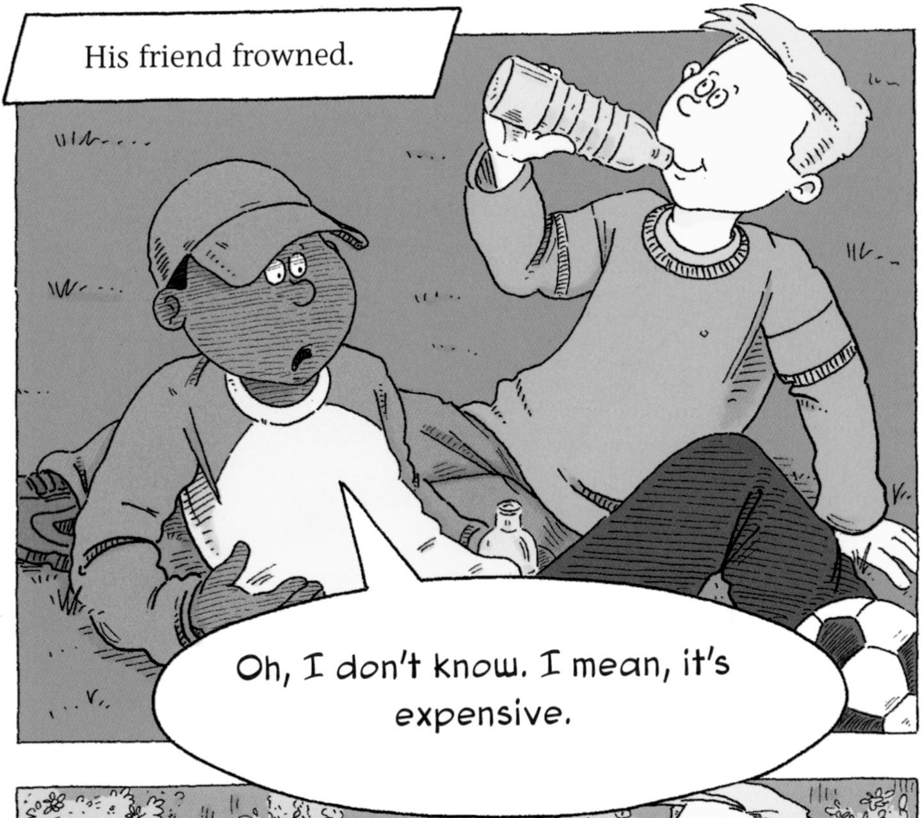
His friend frowned.
Oh, I don't know. I mean, it's expensive.

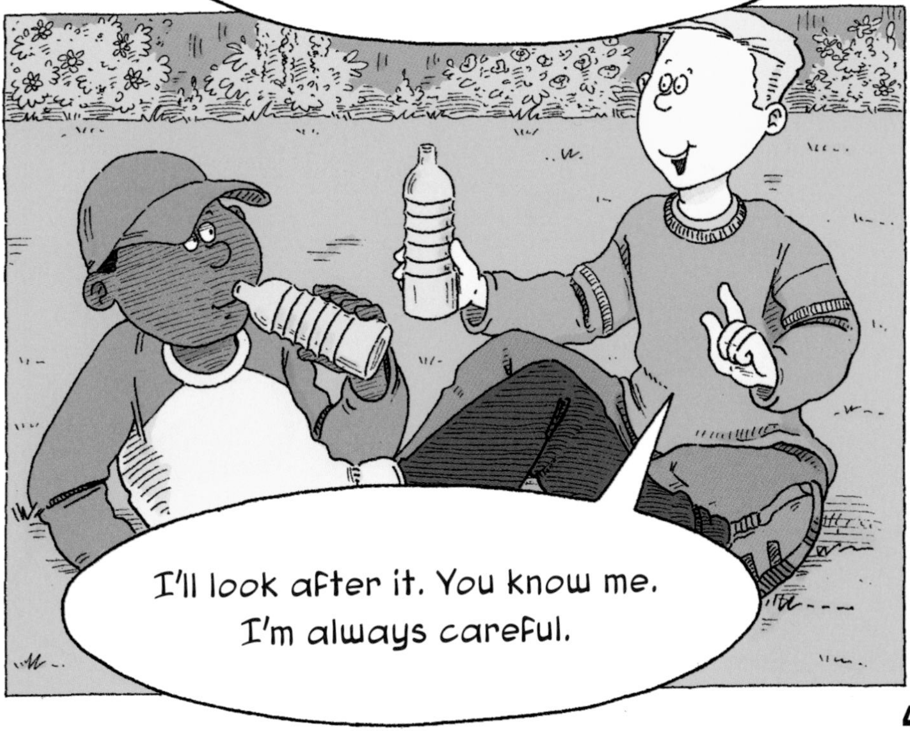
I'll look after it. You know me. I'm always careful.

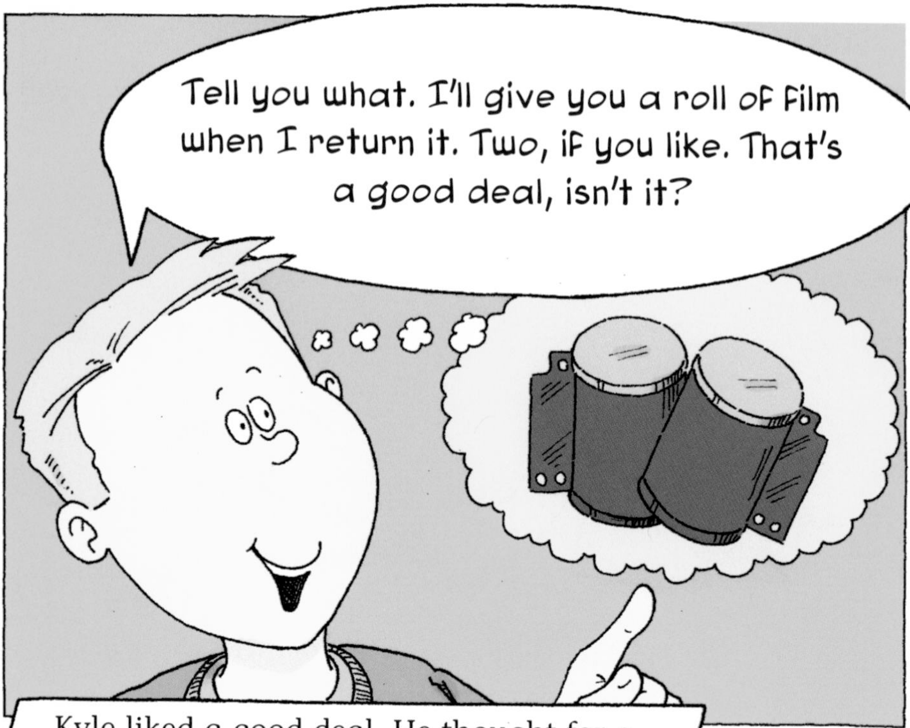
Tell you what. I'll give you a roll of film when I return it. Two, if you like. That's a good deal, isn't it?

Kyle liked a good deal. He thought for a minute, and then he agreed.

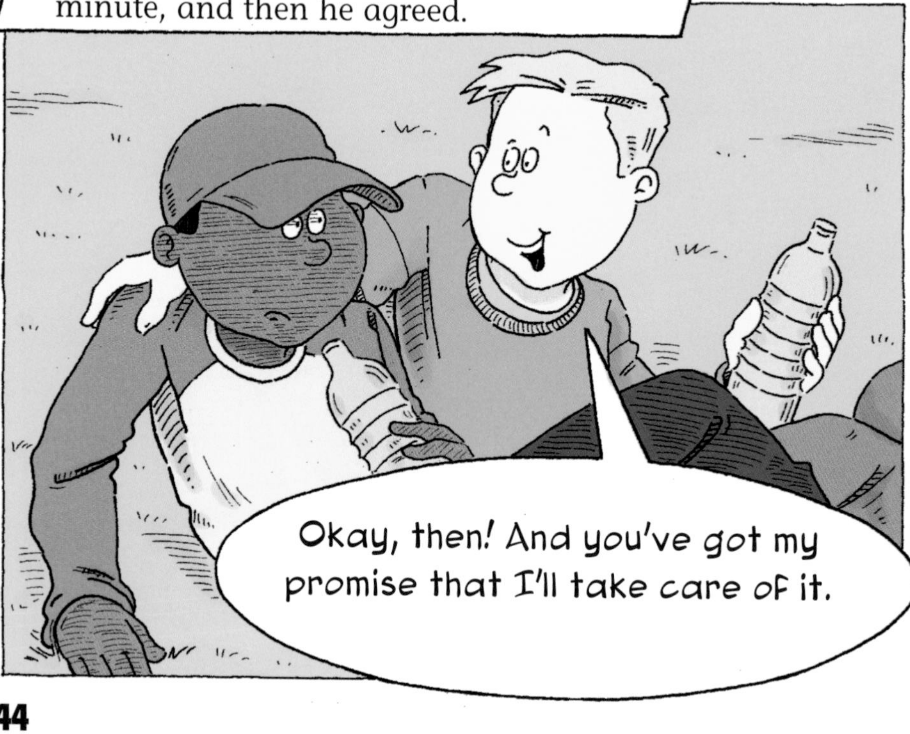
Okay, then! And you've got my promise that I'll take care of it.

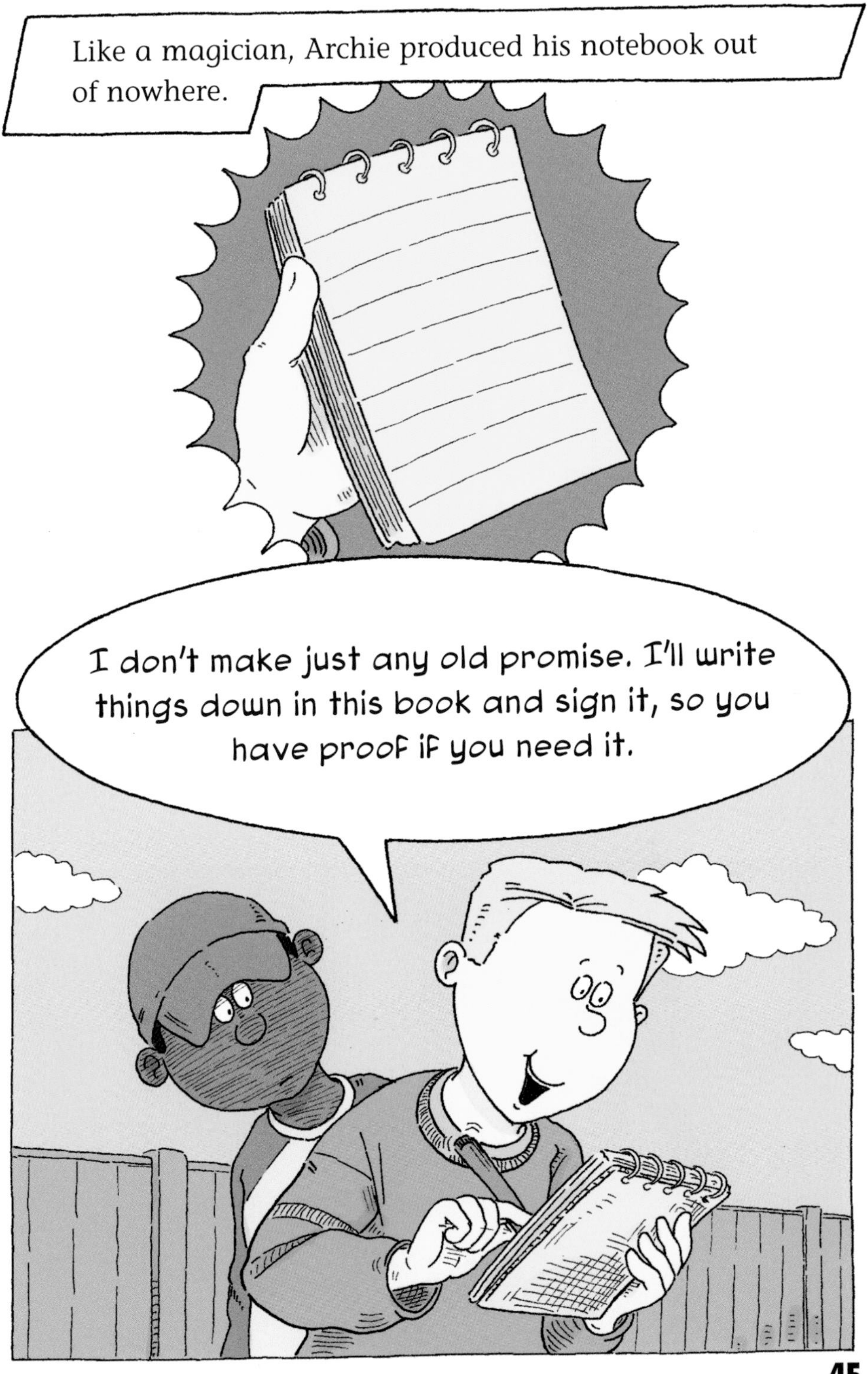
Like a magician, Archie produced his notebook out of nowhere.
I don't make just any old promise. I'll write things down in this book and sign it, so you have proof if you need it.

While Kyle watched in surprise, Archie scribbled away and then added his name. He held the page up to Kyle, who read it and then nodded again.

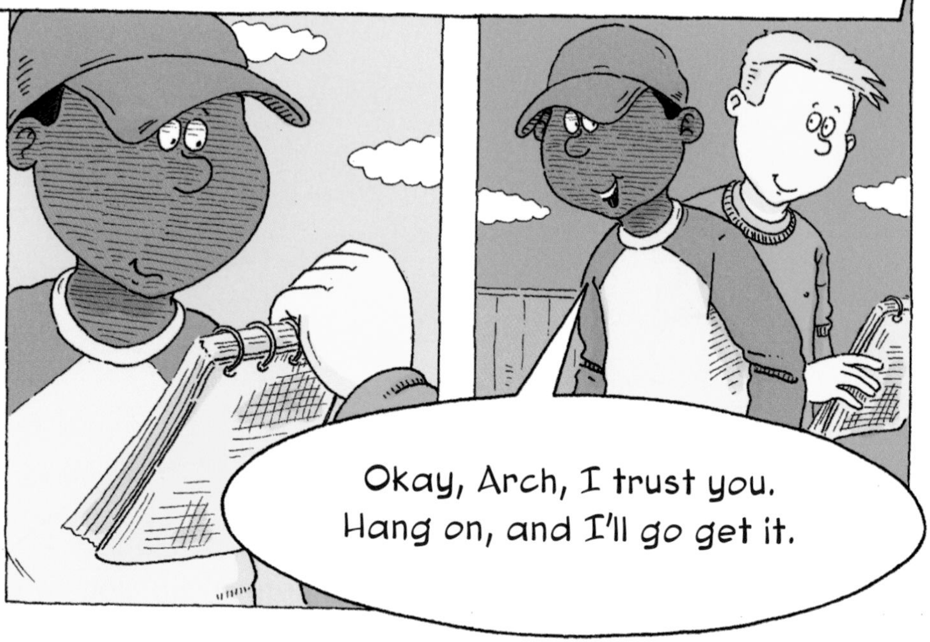
Okay, Arch, I trust you.
Hang on, and I'll go get it.

Archie rubbed his hands together. He had pulled off another part of his plan.

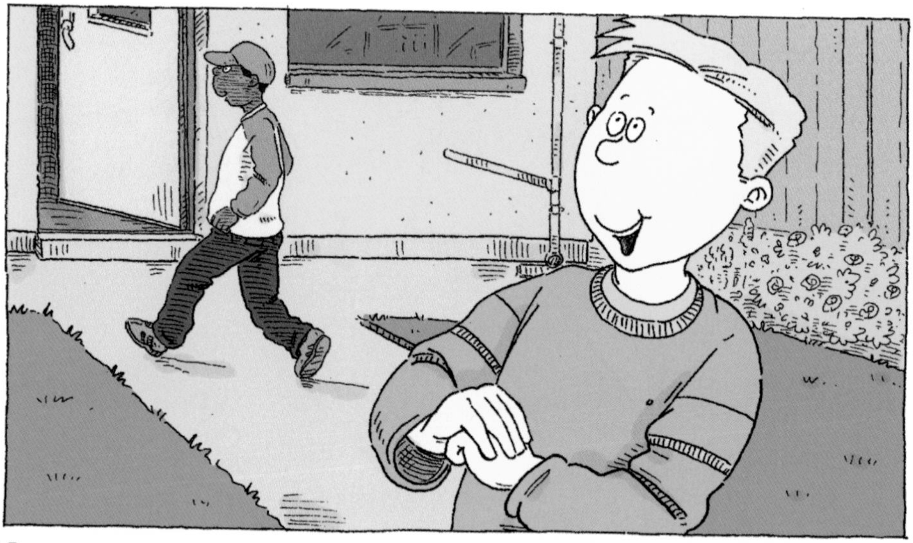

CHAPTER SIX

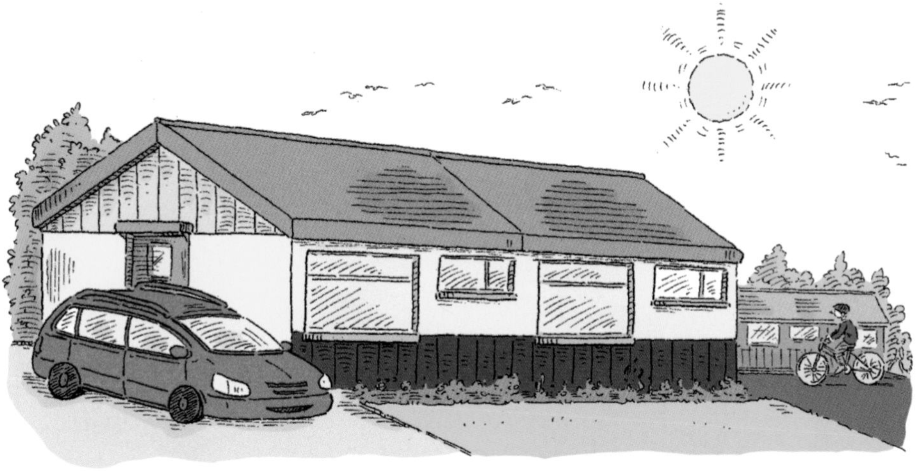

As soon as the family was settled in their cabin at Carnegie Park, Mom had something to say to them.

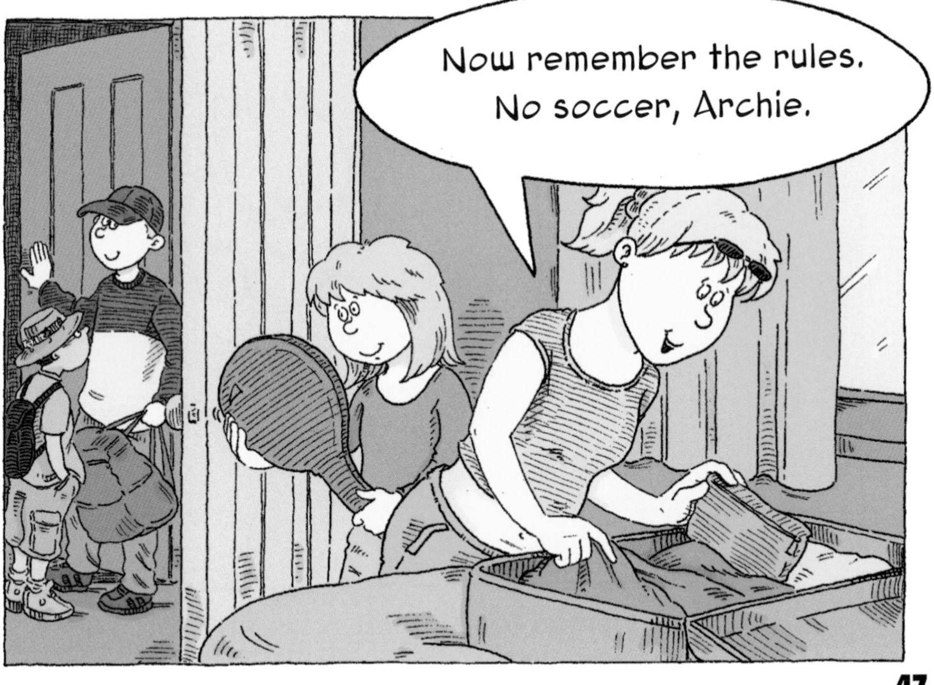
Now remember the rules. No soccer, Archie.

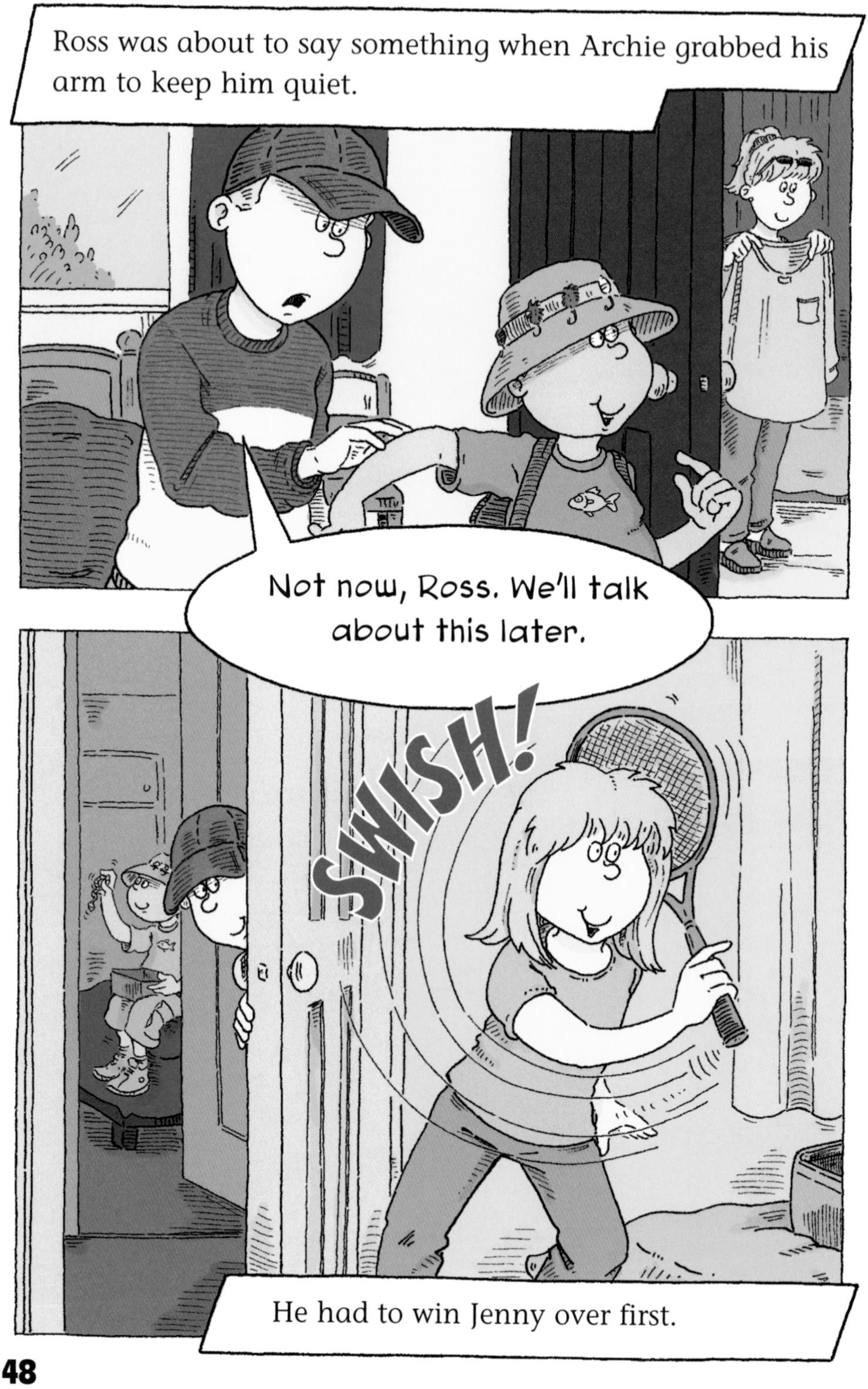
Ross was about to say something when Archie grabbed his arm to keep him quiet.
Not now, Ross. We'll talk about this later.
SWISH!
He had to win Jenny over first.

Archie wasted no time finding Tom, who was heading to the swimming pool. "I've been thinking, I don't —" Tom said, when suddenly, Archie pulled the borrowed camera from behind his back.

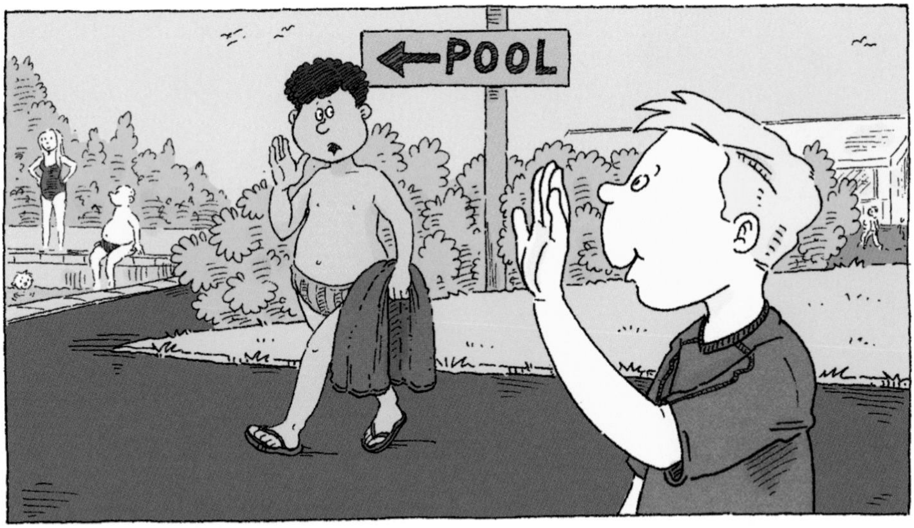
POOL

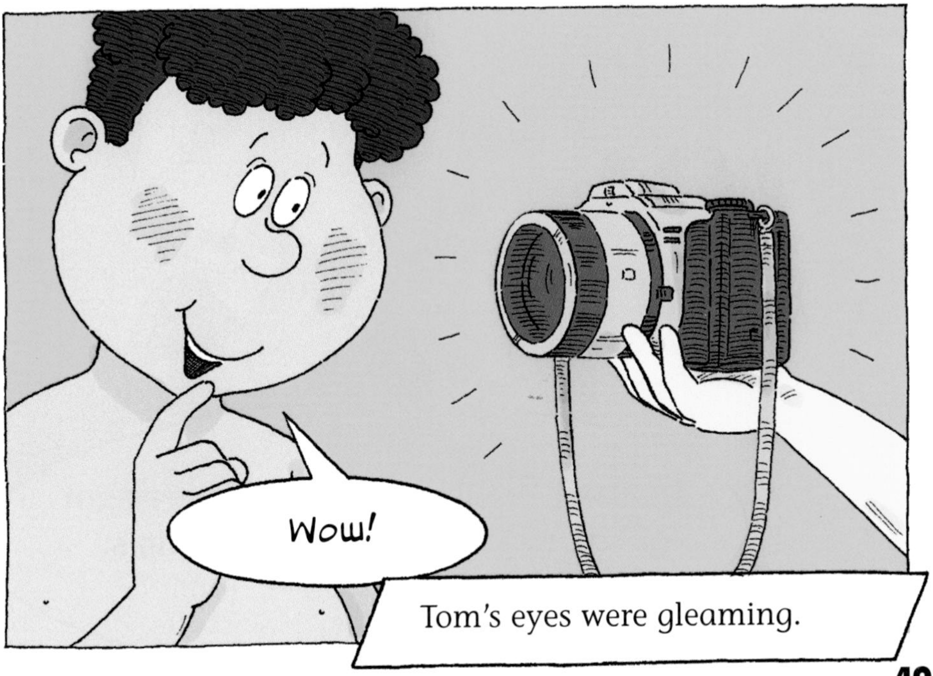
Wow!
Tom's eyes were gleaming.

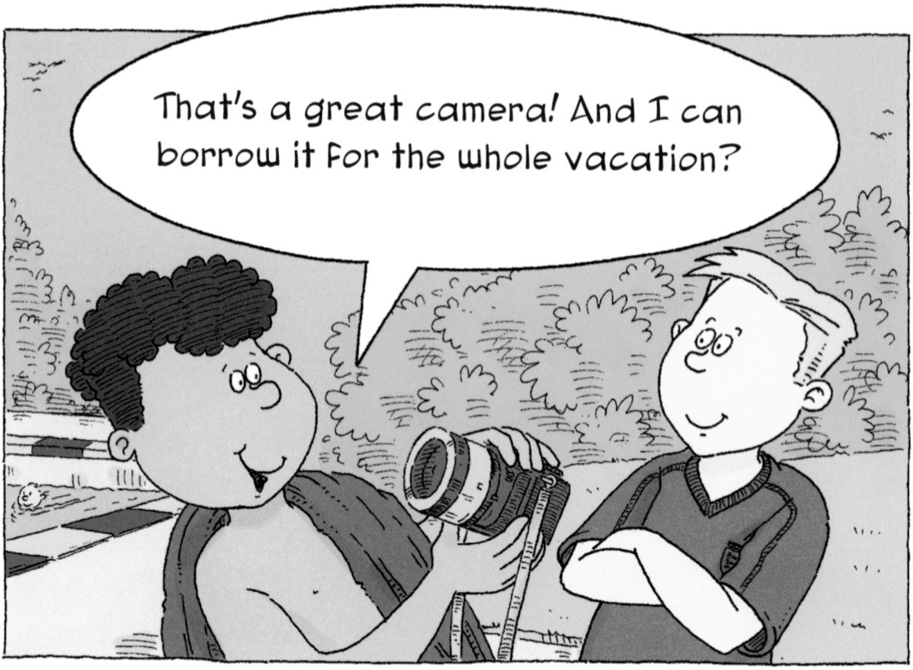
That's a great camera! And I can borrow it for the whole vacation?

"Yes," agreed Archie, pulling out his notebook.

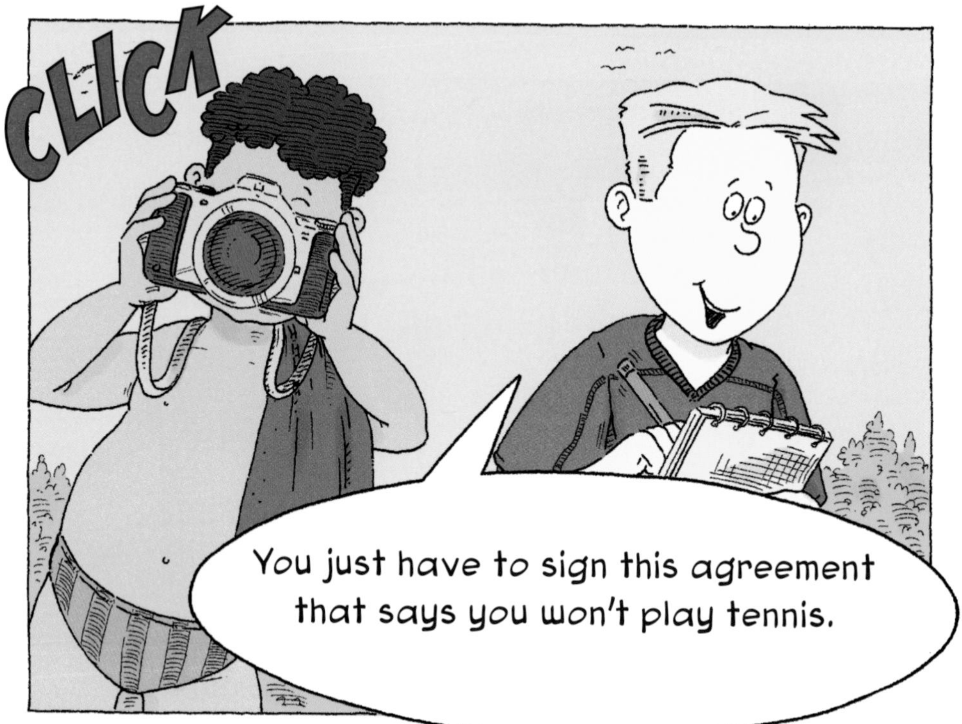
CLICK
You just have to sign this agreement that says you won't play tennis.

"I don't know what Jenny's going to say," Tom remarked sadly as he signed the page.

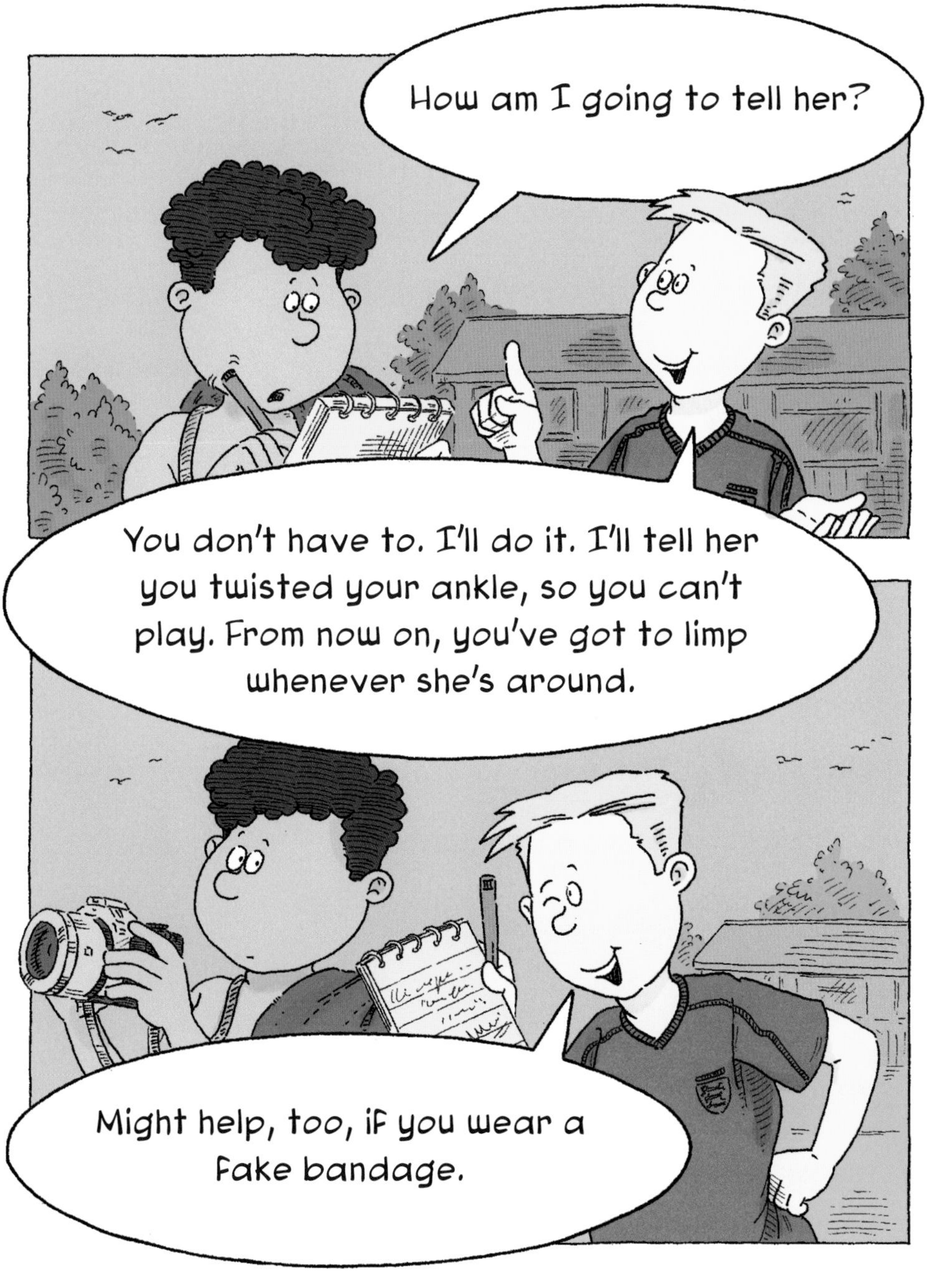
How am I going to tell her?
You don't have to. I'll do it. I'll tell her you twisted your ankle, so you can't play. From now on, you've got to limp whenever she's around.
Might help, too, if you wear a fake bandage.

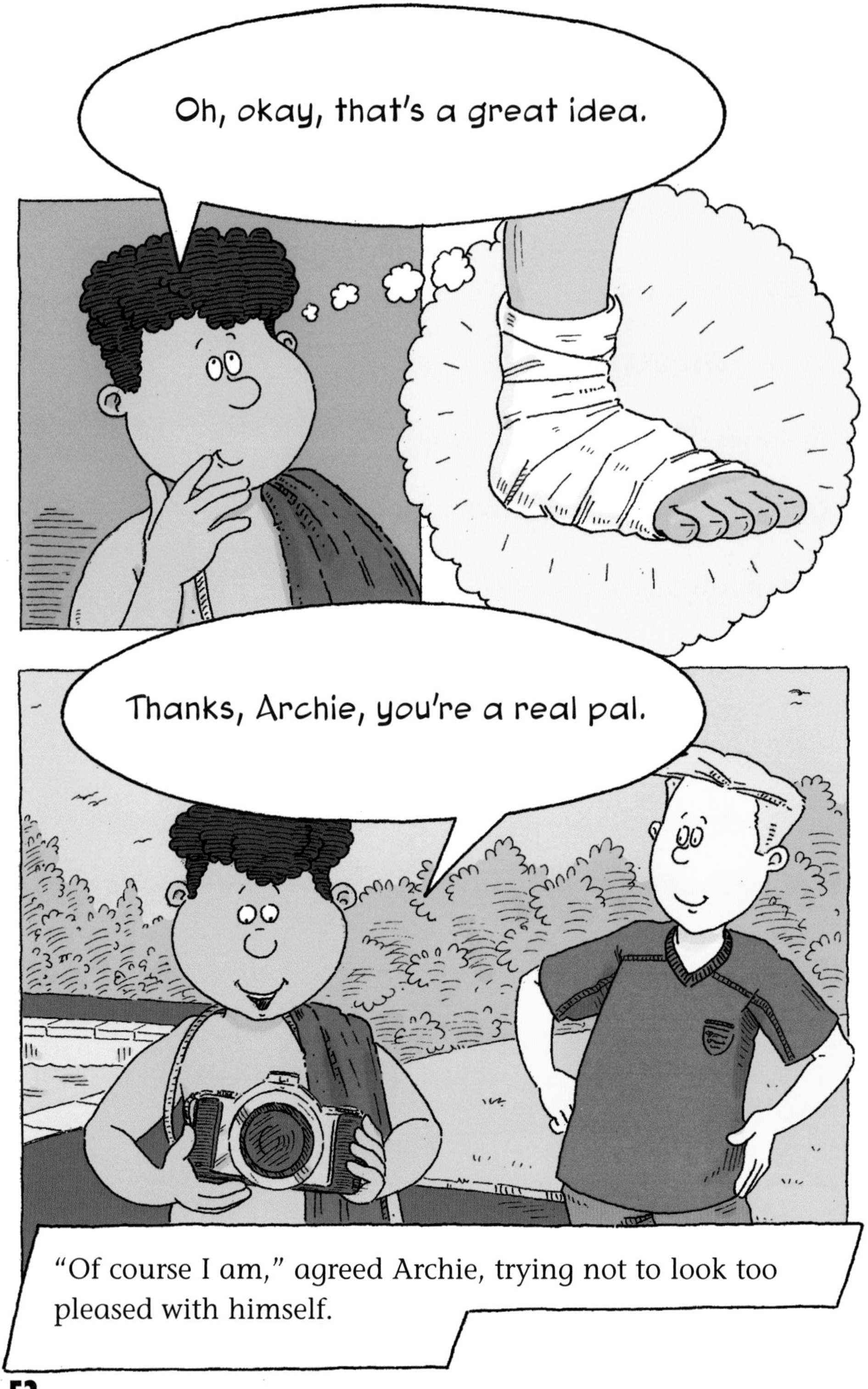

Oh, okay, that's a great idea.
Thanks, Archie, you're a real pal.
"Of course I am," agreed Archie, trying not to look too pleased with himself.

Later that day, Jenny came in from tennis practice and asked Archie if he knew where Tom was. He hadn't been at practice.

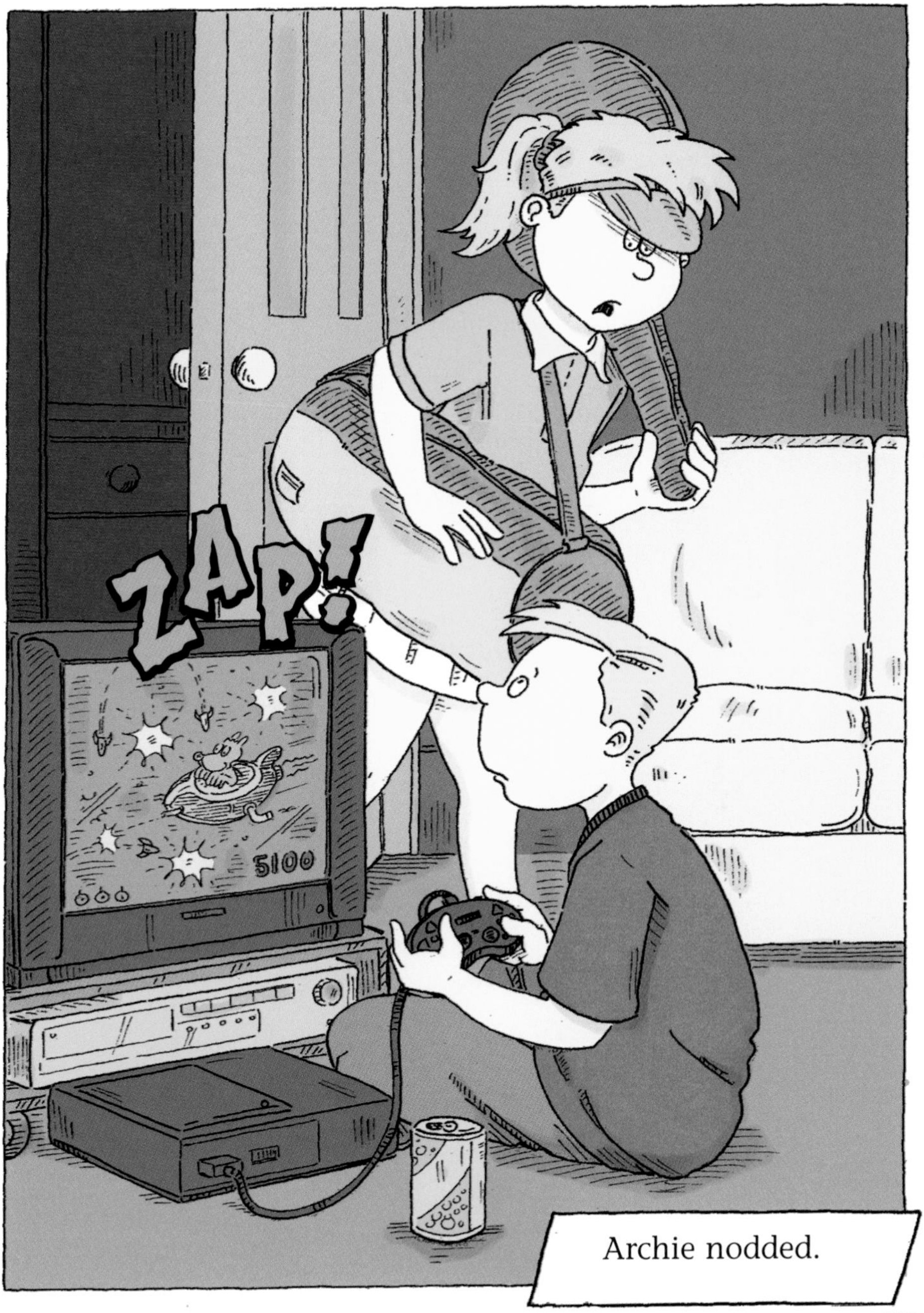
ZAP!
5100
Archie nodded.

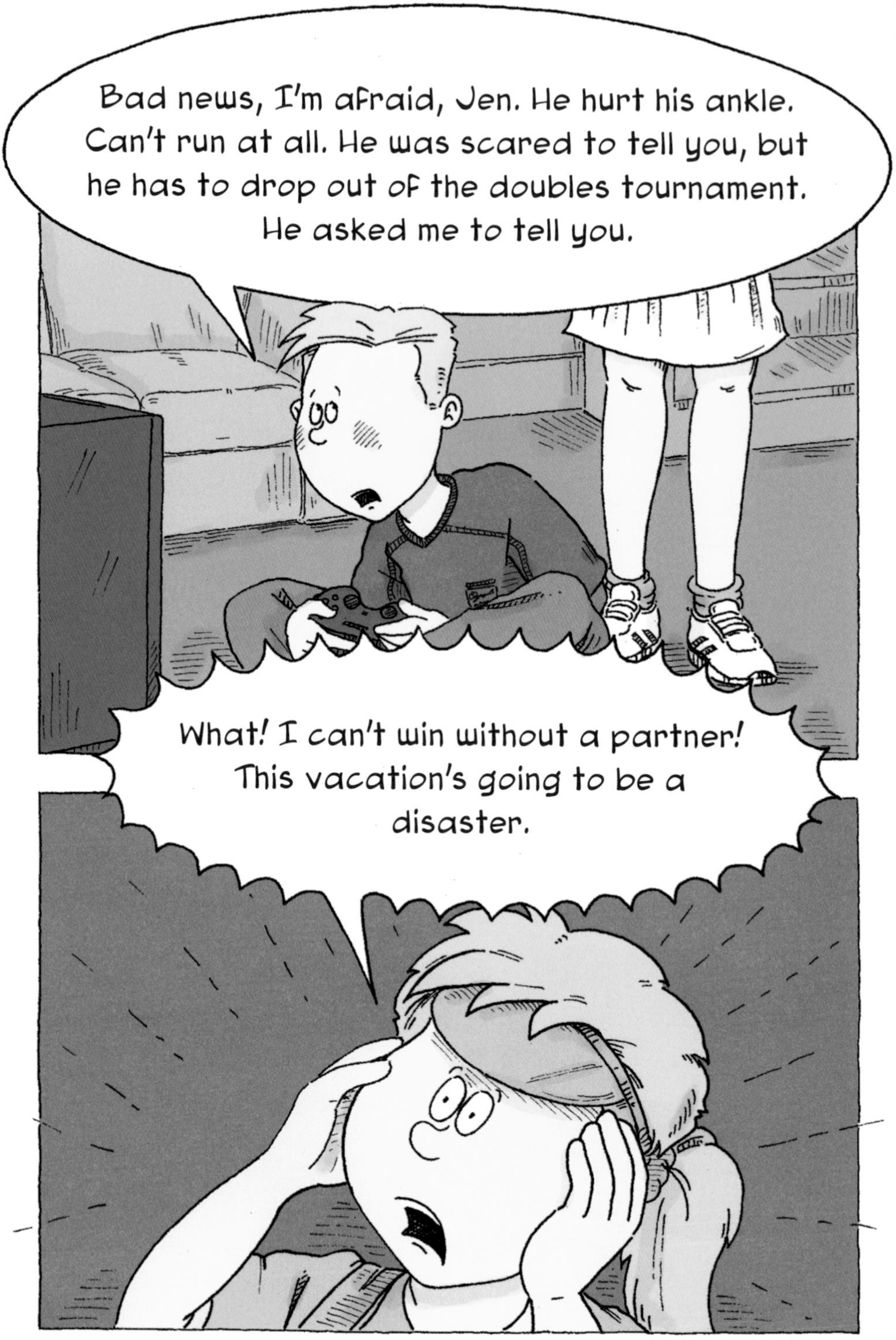
Bad news, I'm afraid, Jen. He hurt his ankle. Can't run at all. He was scared to tell you, but he has to drop out of the doubles tournament. He asked me to tell you.
What! I can't win without a partner! This vacation's going to be a disaster.

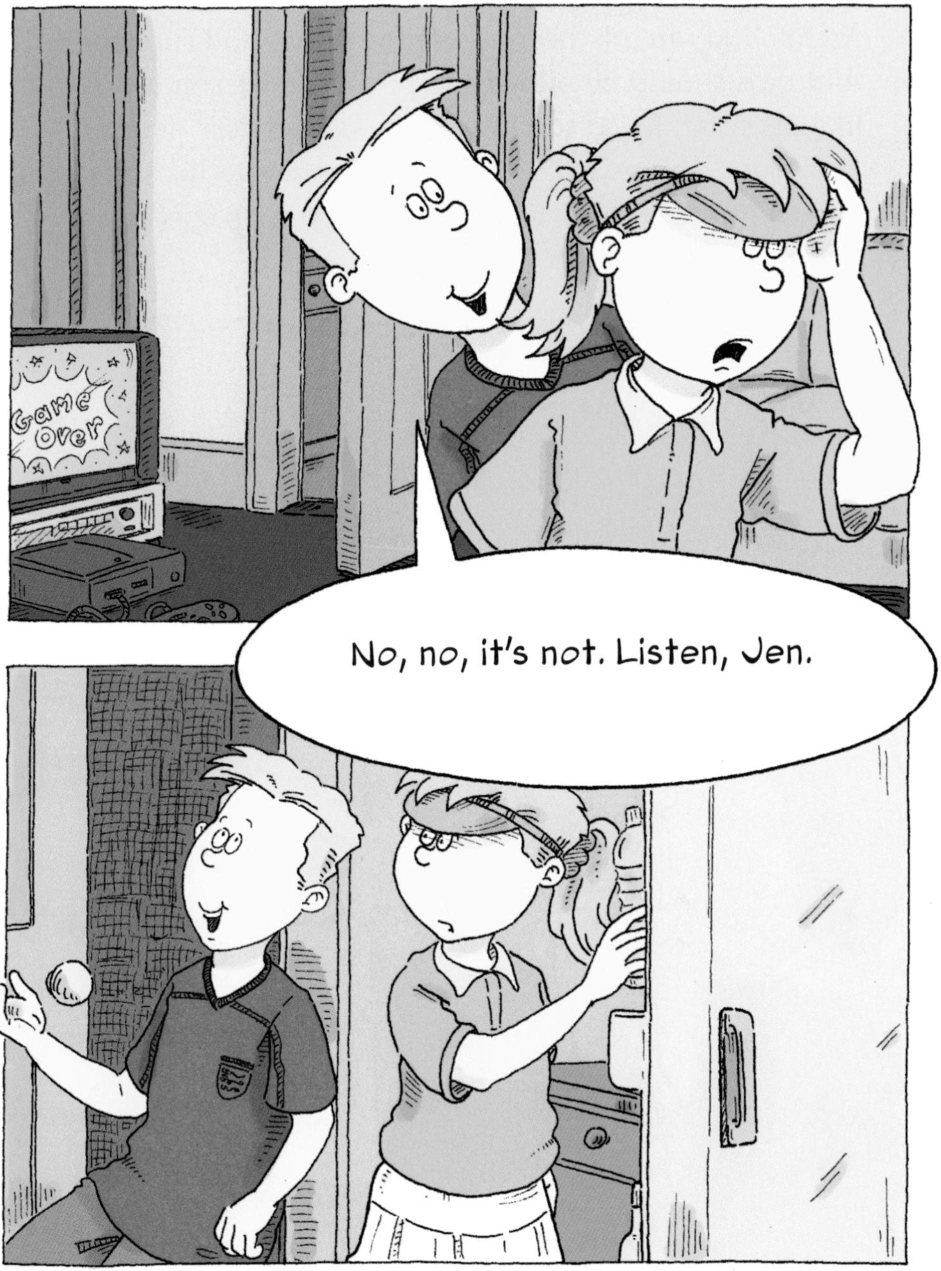
Game Over
No, no, it's not. Listen, Jen.

And Archie told her that he was willing to take Tom's place just as long as she agreed to take part in the soccer tournament.

Archie had already been to see the coach and suggested that girls should be allowed to play because some, like his sister, loved to play and were also very good. The coach, impressed by Archie's devotion to his sister, agreed immediately. He was going to put up special notices to attract more players.

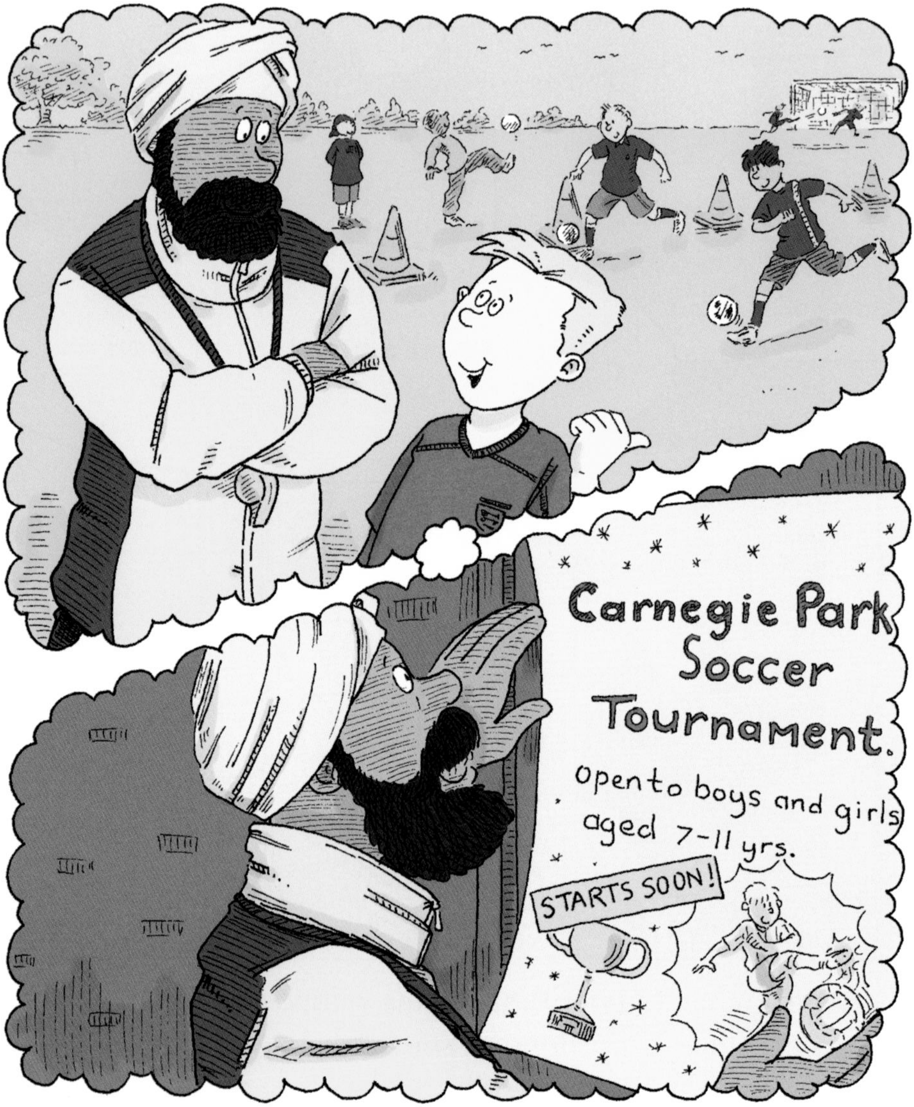
Carnegie Park Soccer Tournament.
Open to boys and girls aged 7-11 yrs.
STARTS SOON!

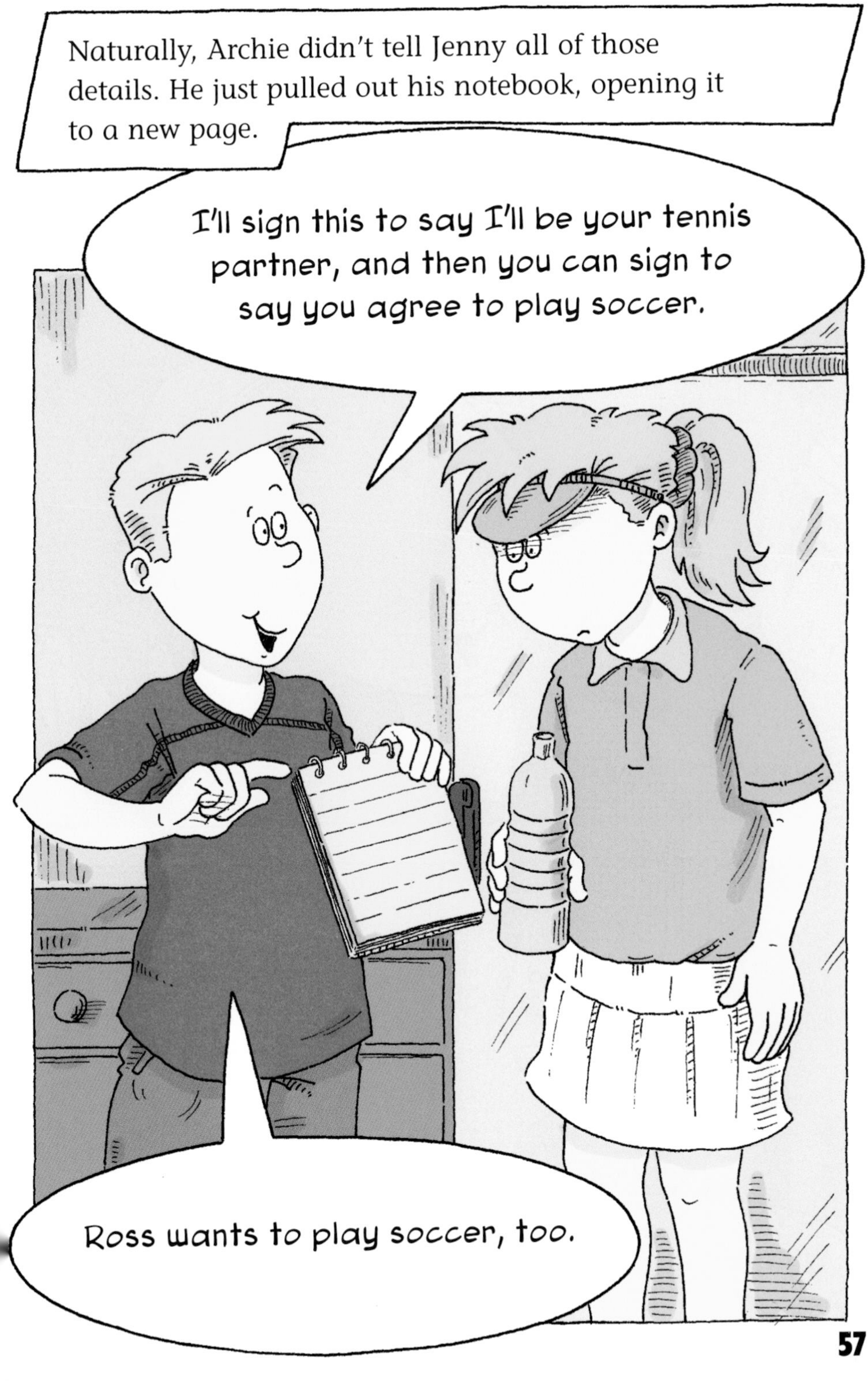
Naturally, Archie didn't tell Jenny all of those details. He just pulled out his notebook, opening it to a new page.
I'll sign this to say I'll be your tennis partner, and then you can sign to say you agree to play soccer.
Ross wants to play soccer, too.

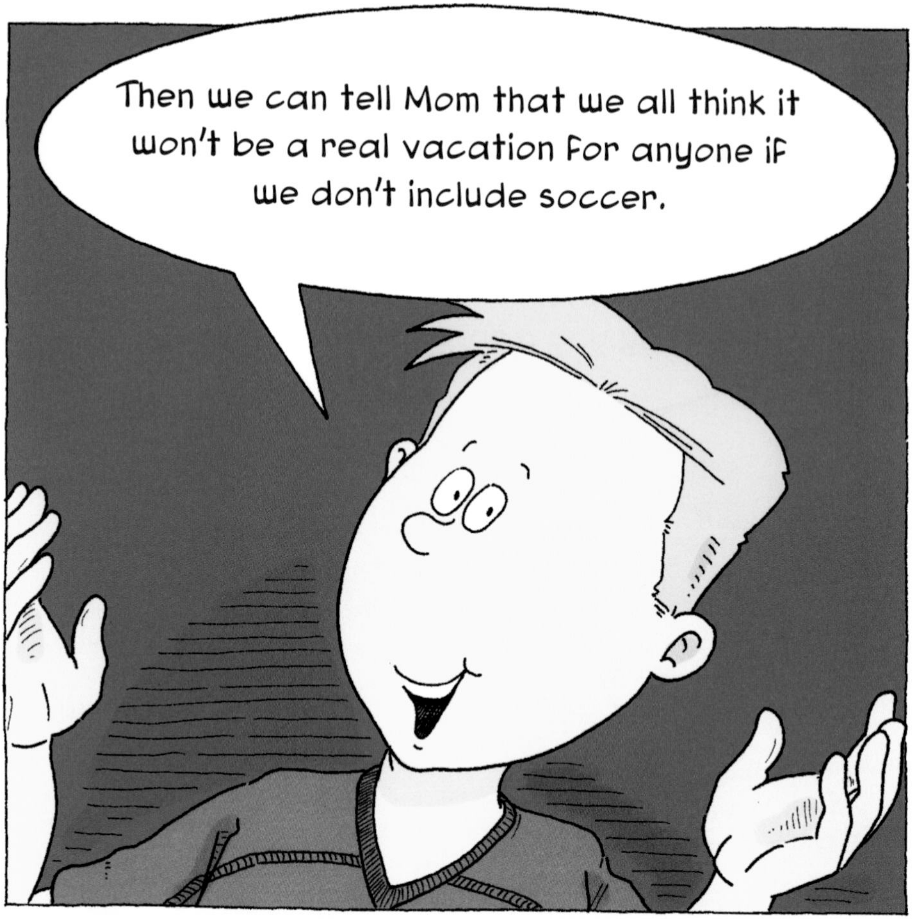
Then we can tell Mom that we all think it won't be a real vacation for anyone if we don't include soccer.

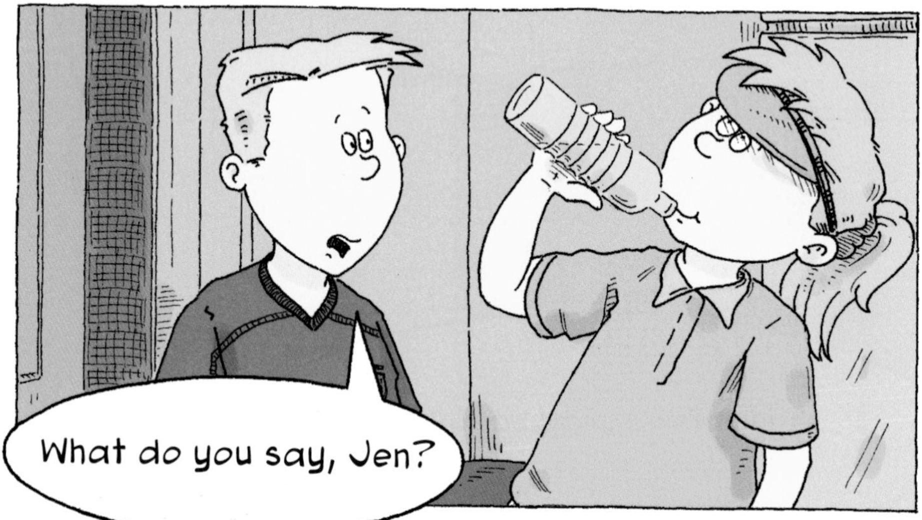
What do you say, Jen?

To his amazement, she simply beamed at him.

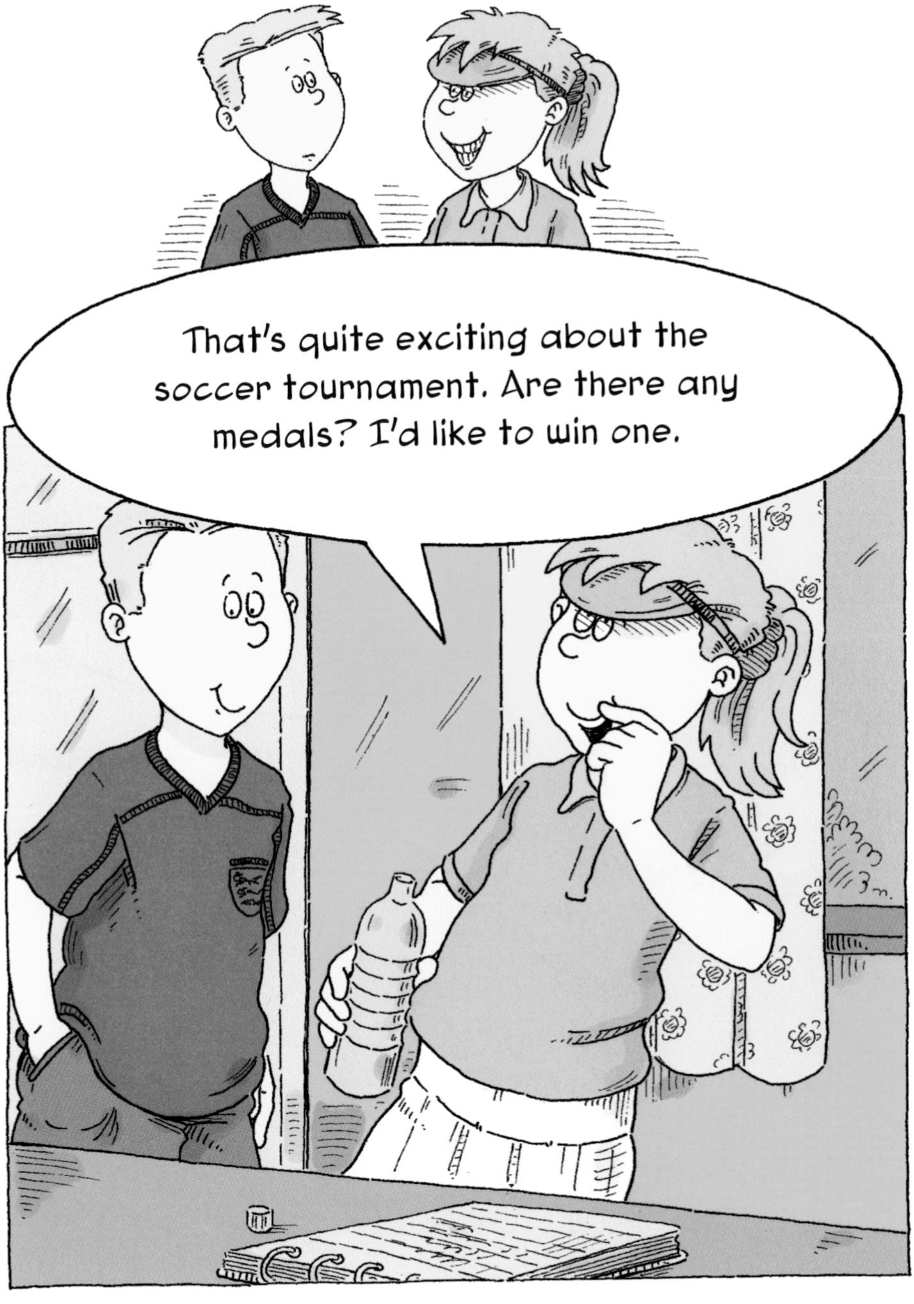
That's quite exciting about the soccer tournament. Are there any medals? I'd like to win one.

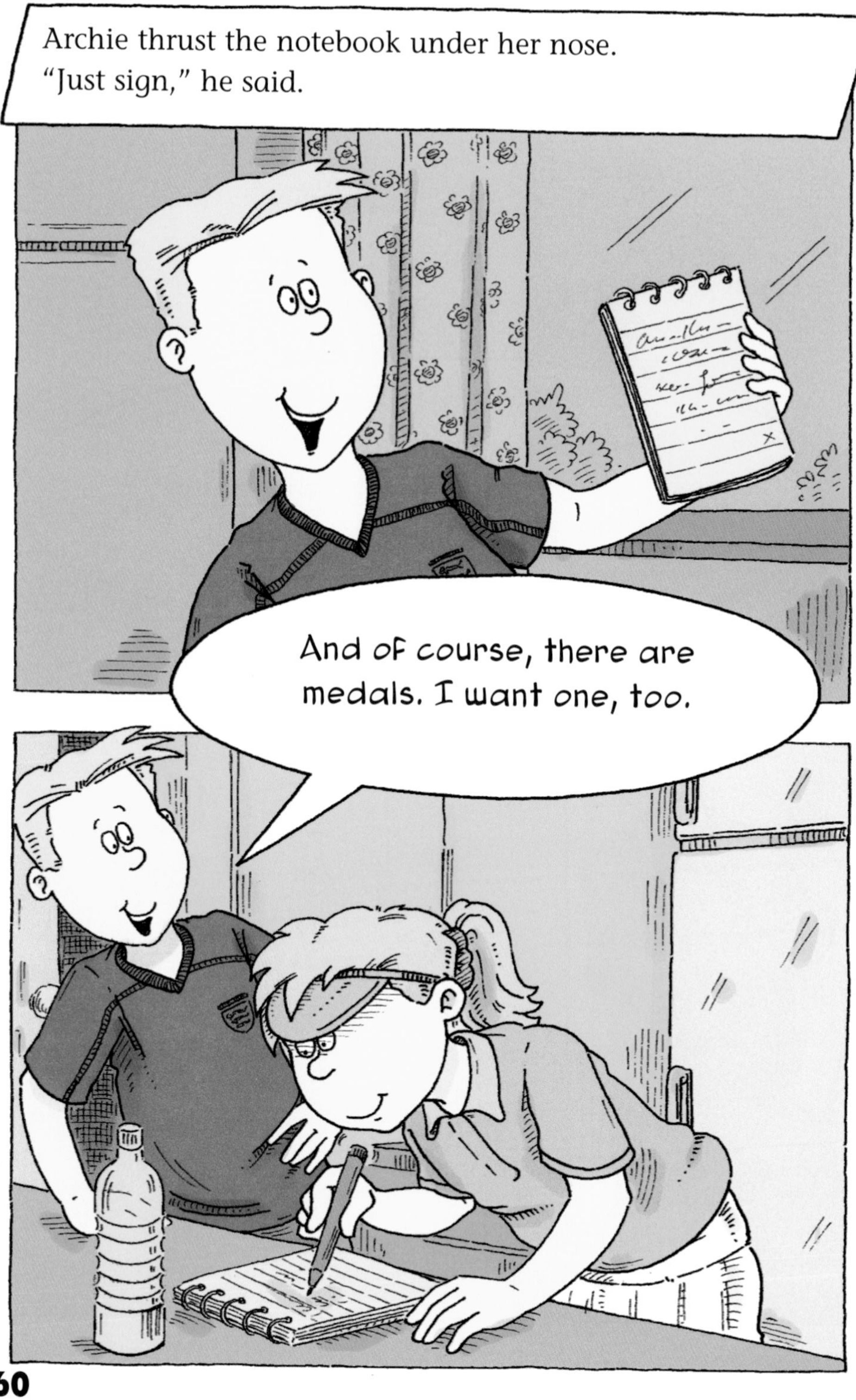
Archie thrust the notebook under her nose.
"Just sign," he said.
And of course, there are medals. I want one, too.

CHAPTER SEVEN

That night Archie tried to decide when would be the best moment to tell Mom what he and Jenny and Ross wanted. She'd probably suspect that Archie had been plotting to get his way, but the names in the notebook would prove that soccer mattered to all of them.

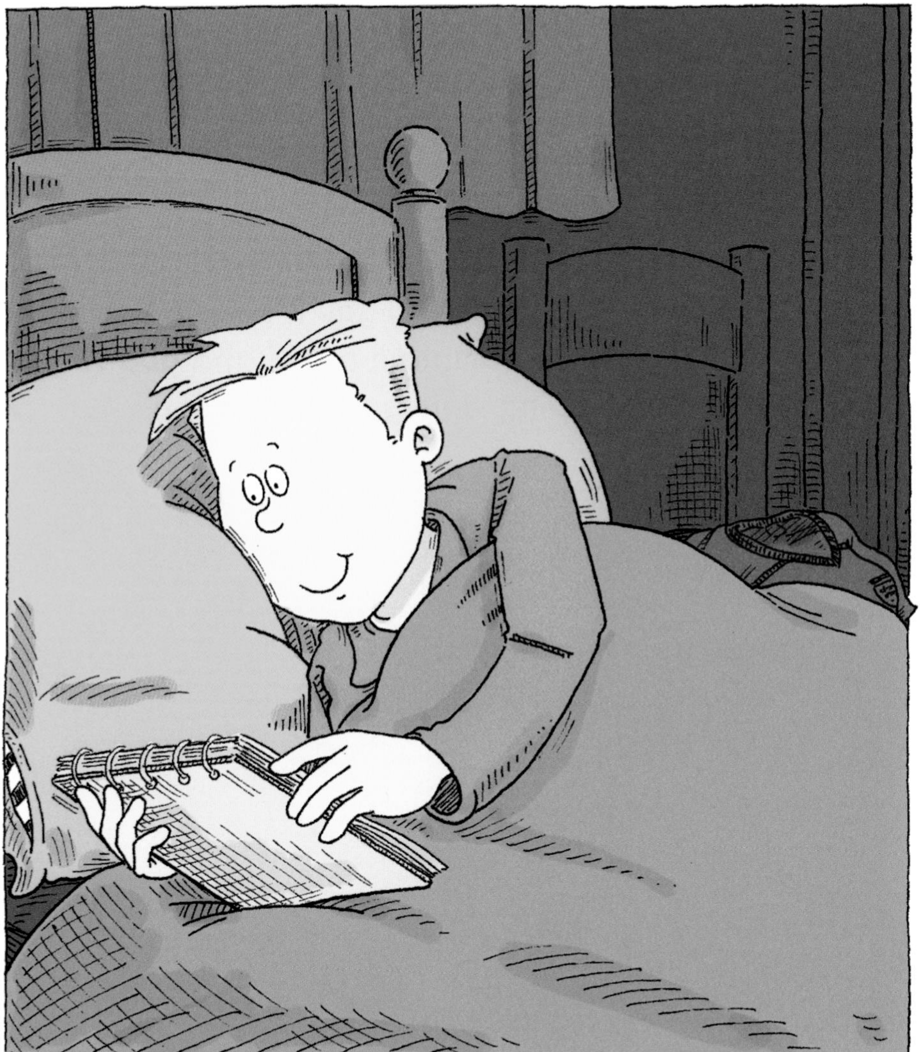

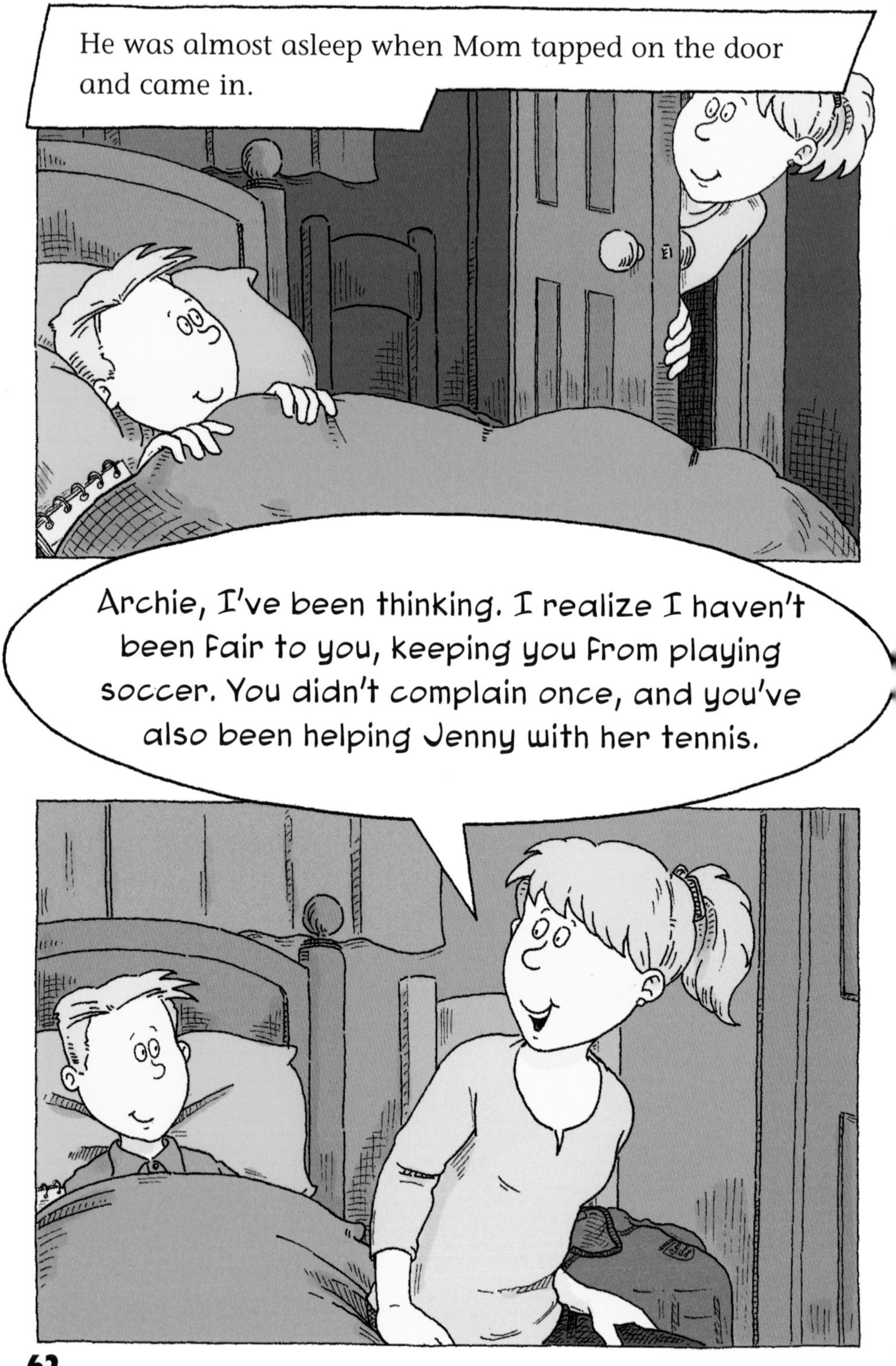
He was almost asleep when Mom tapped on the door and came in.
Archie, I've been thinking. I realize I haven't been fair to you, keeping you from playing soccer. You didn't complain once, and you've also been helping Jenny with her tennis.

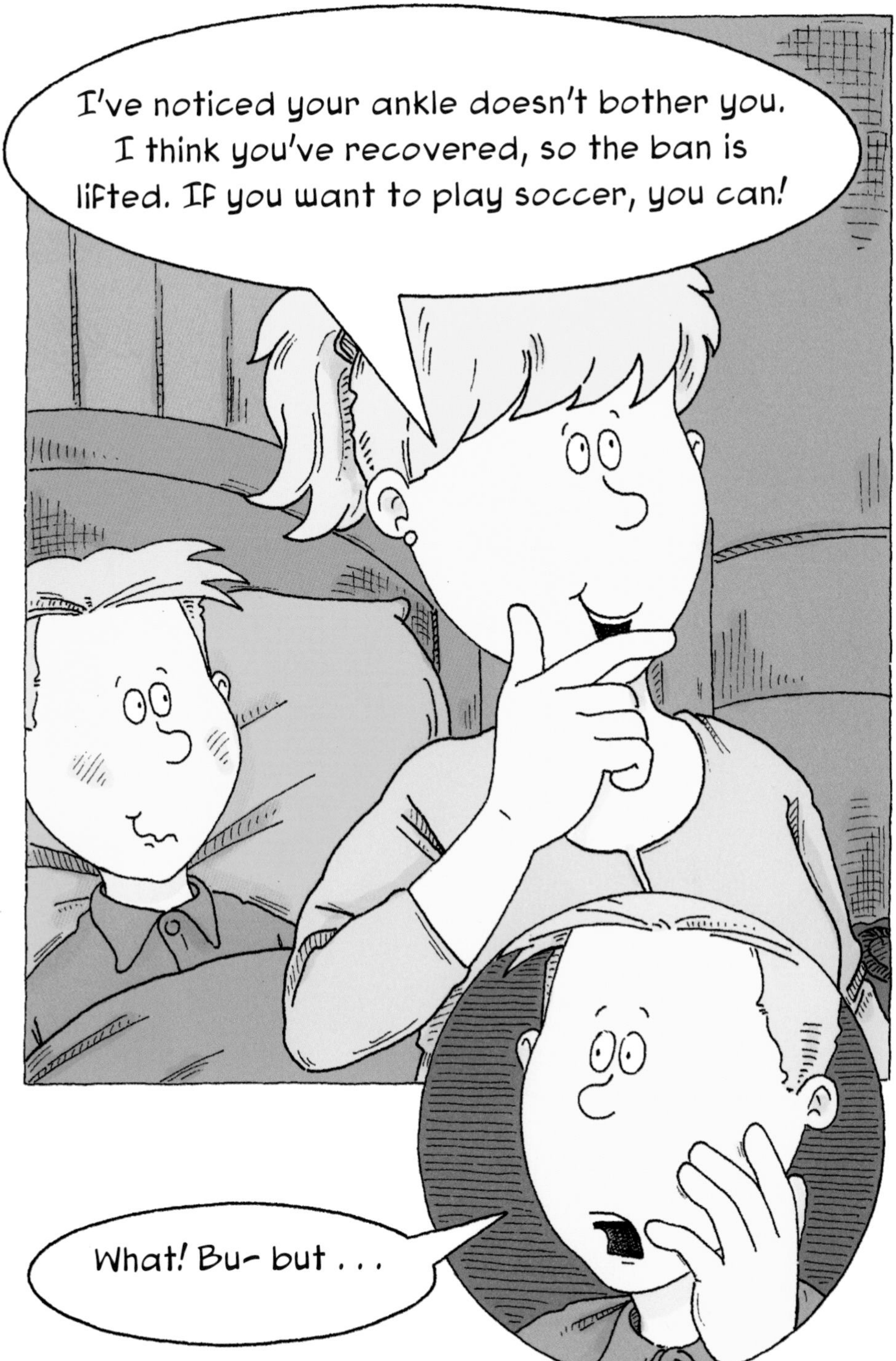
I've noticed your ankle doesn't bother you. I think you've recovered, so the ban is lifted. If you want to play soccer, you can!
What! Bu- but . . .

Archie was stunned. All his clever planning had been for nothing! Kyle had been right all along when he said moms change their minds in time. Why didn't he trust Kyle's advice?

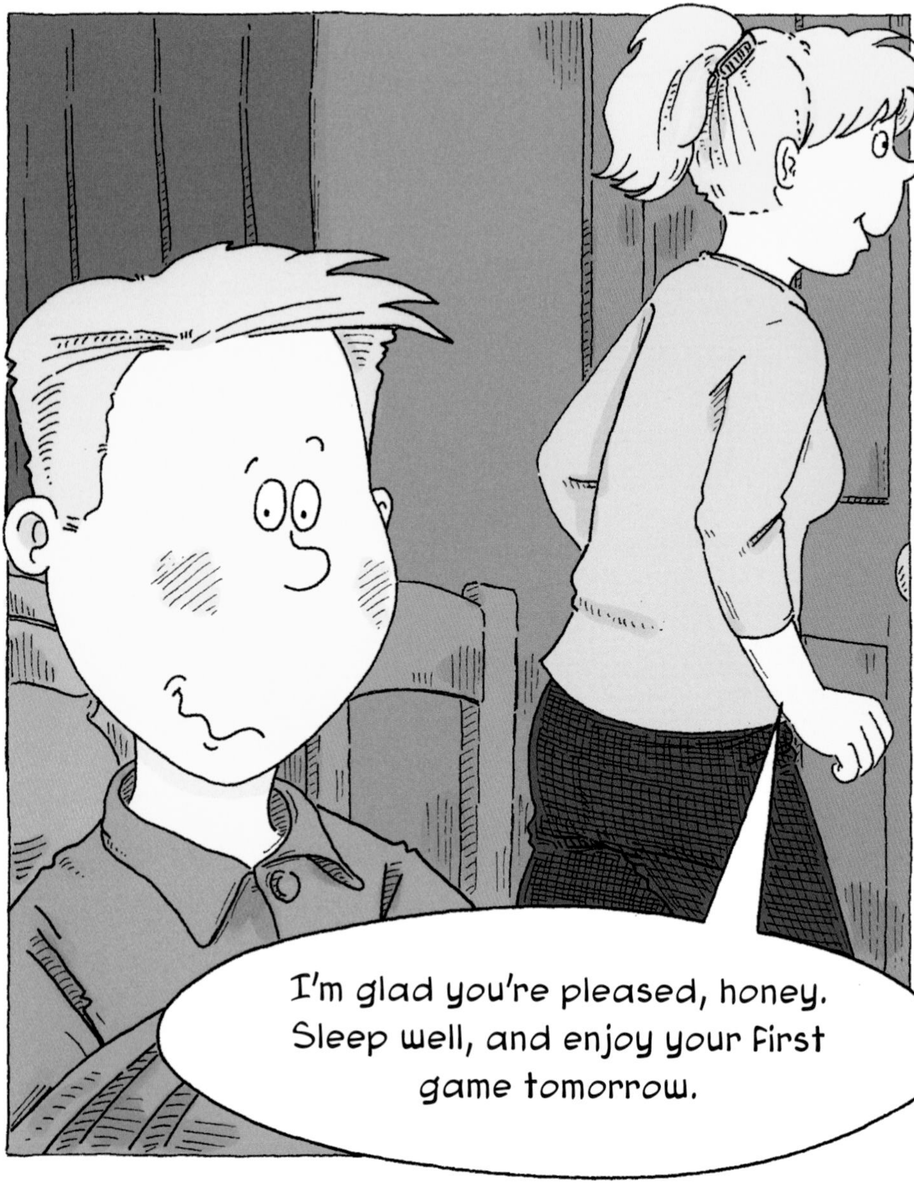
I'm glad you're pleased, honey. Sleep well, and enjoy your first game tomorrow.

Archie collapsed on his pillow, still not knowing whether to be happy or upset. He was getting his way after all, but it would cost him. His mind began to click into gear again.

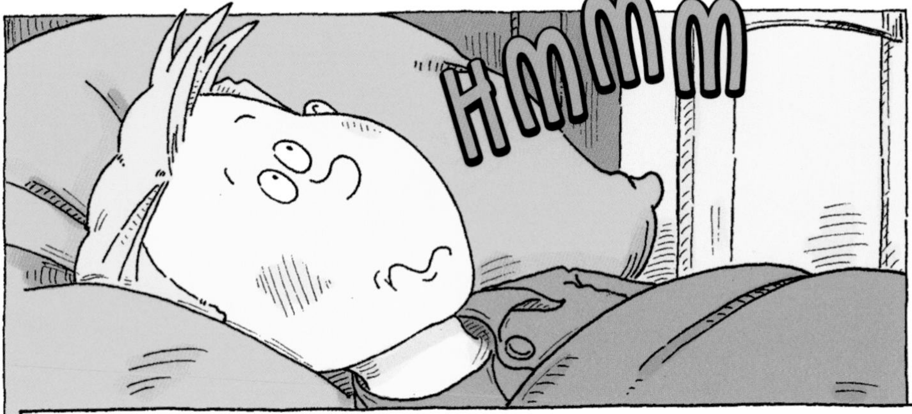
HMMMM

Now he would have to find some way of getting out of his promise to give all those candy bars to his greedy little brother.

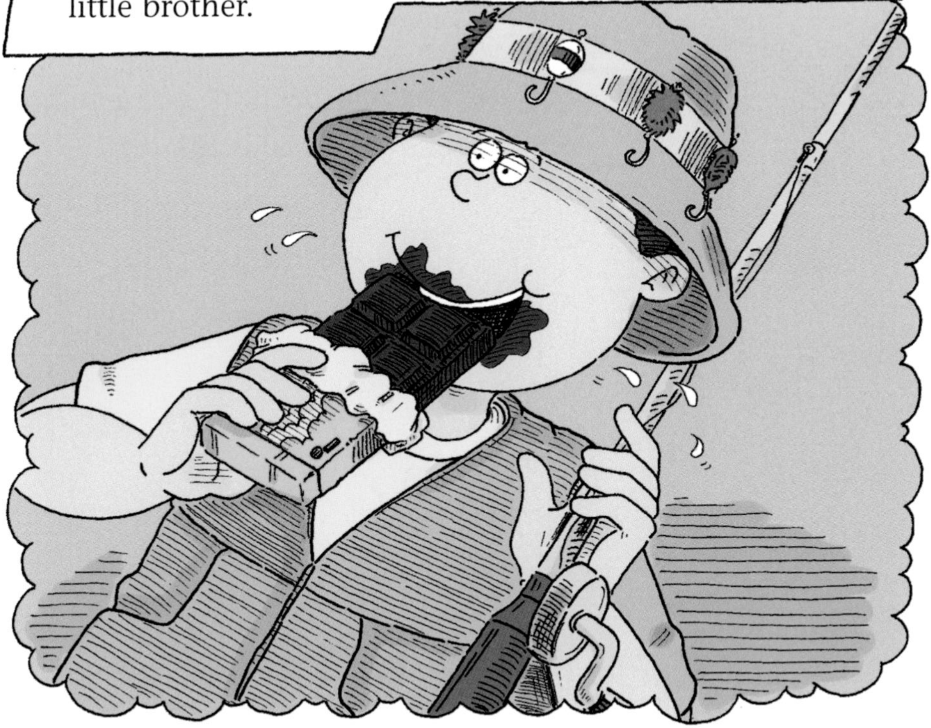

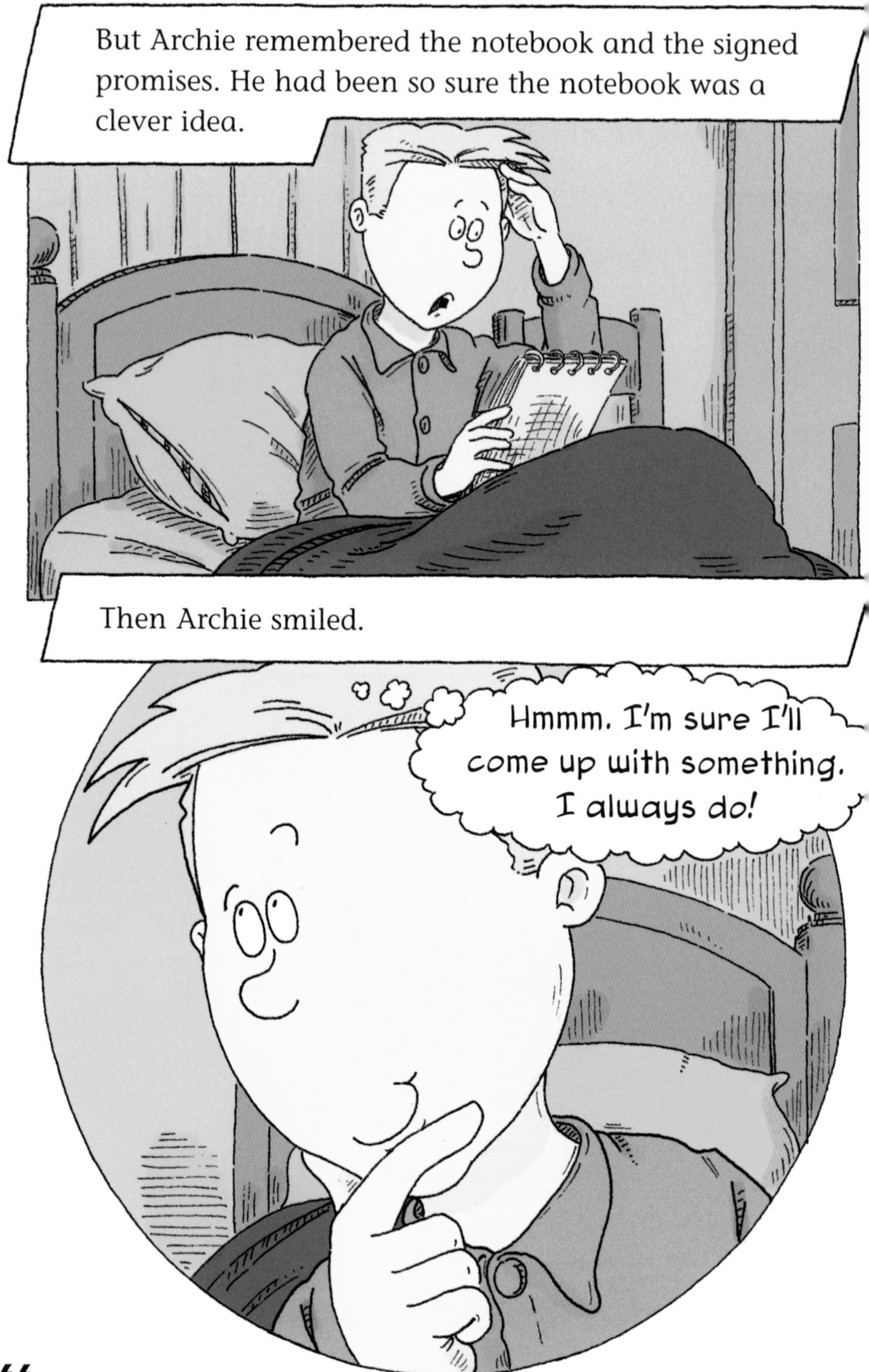
But Archie remembered the notebook and the signed promises. He had been so sure the notebook was a clever idea.
Then Archie smiled.
Hmmm. I'm sure I'll come up with something. I always do!

ABOUT THE AUTHOR

Michael Hardcastle loves sports, and he spends his time writing about sports for children and young adults. He has written more than 90 books.

Michael lives in Yorkshire, England, and loves talking to children about writing.

GLOSSARY

ban (BAN)—to forbid something

contradict (kon-truh-DIKT)—to say the opposite of what someone else said

devotion (di-VOH-shuhn)—showing a strong commitment to something, such as playing a sport

hesitate (HEZ-uh-tate)—to pause before you do something

injury (IN-juh-ree)—damage or harm, such as suffering a broken bone

legal (LEE-guhl)—following laws or rules

medal (MED-uhl)—an award given to someone who wins a contest

proof (PROOF)—a fact or item that proves something is true

suggestion (sug-JESS-chuhn)—an idea

tournament (TUR-nuh-muhnt)—a large contest

Wimbledon (WIM-buhl-duhn)—a famous tennis tournament held in England

INTERNET SITES

Do you want to know more about subjects related to this book? Or are you interested in learning about other topics? Then check out FactHound, a fun, easy way to find Internet sites.

Our investigative staff has already sniffed out great sites for you!

Here's how to use FactHound:

1. Visit *www.facthound.com*

2. Select your grade level.

3. To learn more about subjects related to this book, type in the book's ISBN number: **1598890255**.

4. Click the **Fetch It** button.

FactHound will fetch the best Internet sites for you.

DISCUSSION QUESTIONS

1. At the end of the story, Archie's mom changed her mind by deciding to let Archie play soccer. Would she have changed her mind if she knew about Archie's plan?

2. Archie hopes to find a way out of the promises he made. Do you think he should keep his promises? Why? Is there ever a time when it's okay to break a promise?

3. At the end of the story, Archie wished he hadn't written down all of his promises. Why did Archie write his promises in his notebook in the first place?

WRITING PROMPTS

1. Write what you think Archie does after the story. Does he buy his brother chocolate? Does he back out of his promise? Or does he think up a clever new plan?

2. Write about a promise that you made but didn't want to keep. What was the promise? Why did you make it? Did you keep or break your promise?

3. Archie loves playing soccer. Write about something you enjoy doing, such as working on a hobby or playing a sport.

ALSO PUBLISHED BY MICHAEL HARDCASTLE

HIT IT!
SCOTT'S TEAM IS PLAYING FOR THE CHAMPIONSHIP!
BY MICHAEL HARDCASTLE
STONE ARCH Graphic Novel

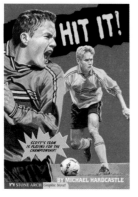

Hit It!

Scott and Kel are rivals on the same soccer team. What will it take to make them work together?

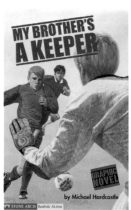

MY BROTHER'S A KEEPER
GRAPHIC NOVEL
by Michael Hardcastle
STONE ARCH Realistic Fiction

My Brother's a Keeper

It looks like the Raiders are out of luck when their goalie gets injured before the big game. Luckily, Carlo, one of the team's top scorers, has a new stepbrother who just happens to play goal.

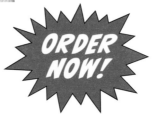